Wrapped Town

and other stories

Jules Horne

TEXTHOUSE
Scotland

Texthouse, Riverside Mills, Dunsdalehaugh, Selkirk, TD7 5EF
www.juleshorne.com

Cover Design: Victor Marcos
Book Layout ©2016 Joel Friedlander

Wrapped Town and other stories/ Jules Horne. -- 1st ed.
ISBN 978-0-9934354-3-0

For Brodie, Emma, Brenna, Thomas,
Alexander, Isabelle and Max.

Contents

Introduction v

Small Blue Thing 1

Raisin Landing 10

Bill McLaren Was My PE Teacher 23

Quite the Thing 34

Holiday Home 42

Reinventing the Beach 44

Radar Bird 53

The Beating of Bread 64

Ally McMahon's New Wife... 73

Loose Muse Walking 89

Wrapped Town 109

Value Families.. 121

The Christmas Chair.. 134

Ruby New.. 145

Disinfected Youth 164

Report 165

Helpdesk 172

Life Kit #1 192

Looking for the Impossible Dance 209

It's A Life 214

Pawkie Paiterson's Auld Grey Yaud 229

The Case Against Wings 243

Agnus Dei 249

Introduction

THESE SHORT STORIES were found in a birders'
box near St Abbs. How they got there is a long story.
Suffice to say that we were surprised to find – in
among the mouldy leaves, stubs of pencil and damp birder
notebook – a padded envelope stapled at the top, and marked
'Do Not Open'. Happily, it had been gnawed by passing
rodents, and the contents fell out of their own accord.

We knew better than to be excited. The days of
discovering a thrilling lost masterpiece are long gone. Today,
so many manuscripts are written, printed, left on buses and
stuffed into odd corners of the landscape that we practically
live in a vast slush pile. The number of readers has been

hugely outnumbered by the number of writers, and readers are precious and rare.

That's why you, dear reader, with this book in your hand, are so welcome and valued. We couldn't do this without you – this climbing inside your head with mouldy leaves, birder boxes, padded envelopes, and all the other props and scenery for the stories ahead. Thank you for opening this book and preparing space in your head. We've got some great special effects lined up, and hope you'll do your bit when the time comes.

As it turns out, these stories aren't new. Most of them have had a previous life in magazines and anthologies, on stage or on radio. But since they've never before appeared all together, and have matured somewhat during their time in captivity, it seems fair to release them into the wild.

We hope that you enjoy them and have had a happy, interesting life in the years it's taken to bring them to print.

Jules Horne (2006)
Jules Horne (2016)

The work of art is a scream of freedom.

—CHRISTO

Small Blue Thing

M ARBLES WERE BANNED in our house. "Can ye no take a telling?" said my mam, peeling my fingers yet again from a small hot ball. She didn't trust me as far as she could throw me. And maybe she was right enough. Marbles were the reason I first borrowed my sister's eyes.

There was this marble craze on at the school at the time. Us wee ones crouched all playtime, clicking our small glass wars across the tarmac. Cheeks and pockets bulging with swirly trophies. You had to be part of it. No marbles, no pals.

But we had a baby. One weekend there was a midnight abduction to gran's across the way. Three days later, I came back to my room to a strange smell. Flowers, soap, new knitting. A glaikit bear sat on my pillow.

It was four months and ten days till my birthday. I wasn't daft.

"Look what the baby's brought you," said my mam.

The parcel of pink wool in her arms twitched. And there she was – a skinny damp doll with fingers and gums and muckle great eyes on her. My sister, Rhona.

"Isn't she bonny?" said my mam. "Look, Mandy – she's got your eyes."

And that was the start of the thieving.

At first, I was prepared to be generous. A baby had playground status, like a tricksy new toy. I had a shot at holding her. Made a few pence by promising turns to my pals.

But soon it was clear that Rhona was just a wee attention-grabber that really ate and really shat and really gret and really got on my nerves.

She stole all my best toys.

"You'll not be wanting this old thing," said my mam. Rabbit was danced into Rhona's cot and clutches.

She stole half my room.

"Stop humphing, Mandy," said my mam. "Share and share alike."

My empire shrank. I was exiled to a rug in the corner.

She stole my attention. After practising the sword dance all week, I came in to entertain mam's Thursday pals. I was poised on tiptoe for the best high cuts of my life. Margot and Daphne cooed as one:

"Aaahhh! The wee lamb!"

But they were looking over my left shoulder, at a bundle in white swaddle lace.

And Rhona was the reason my mam stole my best marble – a perfect blue one with a grand cloudy swirl that I won in a spitting match.

This was no solo job – they were in it together, thick and thieving as they burbled secrets over gonks and mash and milk.

The Banana Splits were on, louping in that daft American way across the screen. It was a bit advanced for Rhona – she was far more taken with the bright baubles I was clicking around the floor. For peace I gave her my best one to hold, and she grabbed it happily in her fist. I was sucking another one in my gob when – oh oh, chongo – my mother swooped.

There's danger in the wisps of a marble. Like trapped clouds wanting free. If you stare at them too long, they'll pull you right inside.

Rhona's cheek had a big hard boil out the side, like a squirrel-wad of chicken soup.

"Open up!" said mam. "Open up!" with that desperate choochoo feeding-spoon voice on her. So Rhona clamped her mouth shut. She was turned upside down and jemmied open and her gums coughed apart, and finally the marble went skiting out across the carpet.

I sat braced in the corner ready for the clouting. And when it came, my sister's honest blues stared in their bland baby way right at me.

All my marbles went in the bucket after that. Not the kitchen bucket, where you could find stuff if you still wanted it, but the outside bucket, where the scaffies came and took things off to wherever scaffies go.

Marbles are hard to hide. Keep them in your sock and you look like you've a goitre. Put them in your shoe and you hirple like your gran. I tried all the obvious places.

My sister's eyes were milky, like her diet, and watery, like her nose. And granted, they were bonny, with their pale sky shine and innocence.

"She's your mam's eyes," said the street. "She's your dad's eyes," said Granny B, against the grain as ever. But I knew the truth.

"She's your eyes."

And her no more right to them than to anything else she'd thieved. I took to searching them when she was awake. With my face up close to her butter breath, I stared, sometimes seeing my face caught in the grey-spoked irises. I watered from the looking, but she never blinked. I grew to wanting them back.

Then came the day I lost five best pals. In the way of these things, they'd gone into a huddle and replaced me with Sandra, who wasn't a marble outcast. By the time I walked home from school, I'd finished howling. But when Rhona's untroubled blues shone back my ugly redness, I'd had enough. It was time to take back what was mine.

Her eyes were smaller than I thought, and sat a bit loose in my sockets.

I blinked. Through the infant blur, I could make out her hands dabbing the air.

Rhona giggled at the new game, but she soon started straining indecisively, and I found my own eyes and popped them in above her cheeks. Rhona stared in surprise, and maybe bulged a bit more than usual, but on the whole she seemed content, in that way of warm milk-soaked babies.

There was a mirror in the bathroom, so I lifted her next door so that we could see our reflections. Mine was disappointing – I couldn't see much beyond the pastel baby mist. But for my sister, it was a revelation. In place of the usual soft forgiving fudge, she met the harsh outlines of bony arms and a pudgy outsize head, all in unrelenting focus. She opened her mouth and bawled.

My mam came hurtling through from the kitchen, and felt my sister's backside. It was dry and unslipping under the fat squash of nappy.

"Shoosh now," said my mam. Rhona's hand paddled treacherously.

"Have you been at her?"

"No!" There's no thinking about the rights and wrongs of lying in the moment before a clouting.

"Cos if you have..." Mam's finger said the rest.

I looked straight at her in the only form of confession I could manage. But it seemed my new eyes were the best liars out – mild, honest, innocent as an angel. Slowly her hand went down.

"Get your coat on. We're going for the messages."

Away from the threat of the mirror, Rhona was soothed into sleep, my eyes held safe behind the veined pink of her eyelids. I walked alongside the push chair, holding onto the handle for balance.

Everything swam, like being underwater at the baths.

We came to a halt by Kerr the butcher's, and waited with Rhona outside. The very smell of the butcher's could make you bowk if you thought about what it meant. Rhona opened my eyes, and found herself right up against a glazed, applemouthed cowhead and a lengthwise half of dangling pig. She screamed.

By now my mam was fairly in one, and with two girny bairns in tow, she sped grimly through the shoppers' legs, me flailing behind, clutched onto the pram. In the end, she lost her patience and wrenched me from the handle.

"That'll do. You're far too old to be hinging onto a pushchair." For a moment I stood anchorless. Neither of us saw the passing Hillman Imp until it jarred to a halt inches from my nose.

✸

"You don't get that from my side," huffed my mam as we wheeled the pushchair into Mr Bryden's, the optician.

"Can you not wait outside?" I said.

"Don't be daft," said my mam. "If you're getting your dad's eyes, I want to know about it."

Mr Bryden sat me into his leather chair and wedged my chin into his metal contraption.

"Don't you worry, now," he said. "We've some lovely glasses for bairns."

He peered at me close, through unattractive bifocals.

As the light went off, I shrank back from Mr Bryden's breath, jaw trapped in the cold steel and eyes shut tight.

"Look at the wee light, now."

I couldn't. Rhona's eyes were wet with tears.

"Do what the man says."

My mam pinched my arm, smiling the while at Mr Bryden in the dark. "It's a stage she's going through."

I raised my lids and stared ahead through the face-cage. Mr Bryden and I and my sister were locked eye-to-eye in the glare of his pinpoint light.

{7}

Mr Bryden was the first to look away. He swallowed, wiped his bifocals and took another look.

"There's something not quite..."

Then he stood up abruptly and put on the lights. Rhona stirred fitfully in her pram.

"Her eyes. They're not..."

Hers.

"Focused?" said my mam. "I might have known. She's her dad's eyes."

"She'd better see the specialist, Mrs Douglas."

Mam bent over to peer at me. I peered back through the haze.

"It's his mother's side, you know."

Then Rhona, her sleep now wearing off, started to wail. She wailed at the bright lights on the ceiling, she wailed at the sharp metal shapes, she wailed at the jagged letters on the walls, blind to the meaning but seeing all with my crystal 20:20 eyes.

"Next Tuesday!" shouted Mr Bryden, as Rhona was bundled out in the pram. "Nine-fifteen! Dr Armstrong! He's very good with the bairns!"

He bent over her pram and poked her belly, as Rhona hunched for another ear-bursting roar.

Then she opened my eyes and looked him full in the face.

Mr Bryden snatched back his finger as if from a burning grate. There, in the soul-mirrors of her eyes, was all the living of my own six years. Something in her expression was too old to sit above those cheeks – a knowledge of school, of sandpits, tig and tantrums. But above all, there were secrets – secrets no cream-fresh baby has the right or the time to know.

Rhona saw his knowing and shut her face on him like a door. We went back home, I clinging miserably to the pram.

Later, while my mam was in the kitchen telling my dad about my eyes – and his, and his mother's – I reclaimed them and washed them with tears of relief to see so sharp again. And my sister's I returned quickly to their place. Too quickly, for I gave her a slight squint which she has to this day.

*

And that would be all about marbles and their dangers, except for one night, much later, when I was old enough to be drunk enough to be a child again. My husband and Rhona's and she lay snoring dead by the fire, and I remembered a game I'd once played.

I looked down, and from my husband's sleeping face, took out his eyes for my own. And when I looked on Rhona, and when I looked on my own baby-stretched body with those tired kind eyes of his, I learned too many secrets I'd not the right to know.

Raisin Landing

GRAN IN HEAVEN, on a pink cloud, dressed in a frothy bedjacket, white hair sprung fresh from the curlers, strumming a diamante harp. Or Gran in hell, charred to a bony frazzle in a vat of fire. Which?

Gran as light, whirling through the sky, wings of gold. Gran as ash, screeching through the sky, a broomstick of dust. How does she travel, and where to? Are there no betweens?

Though what does it matter, truth be told? Either way, she's dead, and nothing to do with me.

Back then, I was six and sweet and pretty, almost, to relatives with a kind and tolerant eye. I wore my hair in bunches, and could play the cute card with the best. There was just one blot on my horizon: a small cauliflower attached to the middle finger of my right hand.

First a bud appeared, then a sprout, then tiny florets that split into more and spread fast across the bottom of my nail. I was fascinated. It was a new kind of spot, to be picked and nibbled in interesting ways. Soft-hard, like gristle from a chicken. I chewed bits off and spat them into my hand. They were threaded through with thin black veins.

At school, a cocky, rat-featured girl called Myra said it was a wart and that I must have been touching myself down there. Down there? I was appalled. Never! I shrieked, and Chinese-burned her wrist until she yelped and recanted.

I was telling the truth, as far as I knew. Down there was territory unknown, to be avoided at all costs. It was indefinably evil, and not up for discussion, much less touching. I'd never even looked to see what was there. Another mouth? A nose? A face? I'd no idea, and wasn't that bothered. But some anxious, guilty part of me wondered whether Myra was right, whether by some awful mistake in the wiping or the washing or the drying my finger hadn't somehow made contact with the skin.

Yet it simply couldn't be. I'd been so careful. It had been drummed into me since I don't know when, and my instincts were finely honed. There are ways, you know. Ways to do all the necessary without going anywhere near the problem parts. Knowledge. All passed down from one generation to the next, by a slap, a look, a sharp tongue.

I embarked on a period of research, scouring all the available books, including some of the ones in the top bookshelf that faced the wrong way, their pages outward, their spines hidden from view. *The Book of Family Health and*

Planning looked particularly promising. I hadn't realised my parents were that organised, or that families were something which needed to be planned at all. But I suppose they were busy people, in their own ways, and father only had two weeks' holiday a year.

The pull-out pictures were most useful. With the skinned man and the skinned lady spread out before me, his colourful arteries and her colourful muscles spectacularly exposed, I pored over their whats and whereforealls, and found nothing to support Myra's remark, and plenty to further my own education. Touch was the key, yes – but touch of hand on hand, not hand on pouch or dangle.

My other reading was *The Book of Bedtime Tales*. From that, among the insipid princes and pixies, I gathered that of all the exotic beings that walked the world, the wartiest was the witch. Warts hung and clung from every bump of their noses, every joint of their fingers, like small bunched fruits or mislaid bogles. But by a quirk of fate, they had the ability to ditch their weird glamour, lose the growths, smooth the wrinkles and magic themselves into something more suited to the conventional beauty ideals of the time.

If I'd touched a pouch or dangle, I would know. If I'd touched a witch, I might not. I could be meeting and brushing past them every day, without the slightest warning.

It's fair to say that I'd had my suspicions about Gran all along. The final confirmation came from one of those late-night arguments that used to drift upstairs when mum and dad thought I was asleep. They were usually fairly one-sided affairs – a long maternal monologue batting ineffectually against a silent paternal punchbag. On this particular evening, we were being treated to variations on a theme of mother-in-law. After a half-hour crescendo, the door slammed open, and a screech flew out on venomous wings.

– Witch!

Suddenly, everything fell into place: the rows of crystal bottles on the dressing table; the enormous ruby snake-topped jars that glugged and bubbled in the linen press; the straw dolls that stood on the shelf, never to be played with; the stalk-legged giraffe that guarded the fireplace; the ribboned bags of blue seeds that swung from every door handle. And while there was no sign of a cat, there was always the fat, sleek Blacky, who pecked raisins straight from Gran's hand, and sat watchfully on the windowsill, yellow eyes blinking.

I doubt many other people knew. She certainly didn't dress the part, preferring cream and turquoise to ageing black, and her skirts stopped resolutely at the knee. Her only hat was squat and woolly, and her only nose was snub.

I never heard it mentioned again, and I was reluctant to question my mother, aware that it was probably a matter of major family embarrassment, like Uncle Donald's hairpiece.

So by the time it came to our next, rare, visit, I was bursting with curiosity. And, with the cauliflower now taking root in a second finger, I also had a few bones to pick.

★

Gran lived in North Berwick, miles away by the seaside, on a treeless, cheerless road full of houses diluted grey by the relentless cycle of sea and rain.

Hers was the loudest door in the street – a screaming saffron that really belonged in another country entirely. I wondered if the yellow was another sign, like the brass knocker on the door, which glared down at us with the face of a glowering lion.

I was ready to do battle, thrust my lumpy finger under her nose, fix her with a knowing stare and say "let's do business". She'd sweep me inside, gripping my arm with her painted talons, and hiss "not a word" from the side of her mouth, out of my mother's earshot. In the meantime, I'd embroidered her into someone taller, more exotic, with a floor-length frock and rings on every finger.

But as I soon as I saw her, my conviction evaporated. Somehow, she'd shrunk, to dimensions even smaller than I remembered. She looked cold, old in the salty wind, her cheeks drawn, her eyes duller. She hurried us in and shut the door, hugging us in her abrupt way, more fiercely than usual, as if to make up for all the missed hugs in between. With my cheek crushed against the shiny stuff of her blouse, I felt her hands – long, elegant hands – pat my back for longer than was strictly necessary.

Mum, with her usual efficiency, had brought a marshmallow traybake, and went off to clatter in the kitchen. I clambered onto the settee and sat there, watching and waiting, my elastoplasted finger prominently on display.

Gran didn't disappoint. Her powers of observation were uncanny. She knew about the wart before I even mentioned it.

"Give us a look, then," she sighed, polishing her glasses on her blouse in a business-like way.

I took off the plaster to show her, wincing for extra dramatic effect as I yanked a stuck bit of dried-on cotton from the weeping wart. I was painting it white every night with acid from a small brown bottle. It seemed to thrive on it, and now bulged ostentatiously, like a clump of rice krispy.

Gran sucked her breath between her teeth.

"It'll be sore, that," she observed.

"I'm used to it," I said, carelessly.

I scraped off the layer of acid to show her the milky, air-starved skin underneath. The curds had fattened out, and now spread right across the base of the nail and up the other side.

Though she tried not to show it, Gran was clearly impressed with her handiwork.

"Where did you pick that up?"

As if you didn't know, I thought, viciously, suspecting that with mum nearby, telepathy was the best option.

She tutted and poked at my hand.

"That's a beauty, mind. Near as big as mines."

I looked at her hands. Her fingers, though wrinkled, were long, pink and elegant, with not a lump in sight. She must be talking about her other hands, the witch ones – the ones she wore when no one was around to see.

"Here. And here. And a wee one there. Joined up thegither. Devils, they are. No sooner they're off one finger but they're hopped to the next."

"Where did they go?" I asked. *I've got you now. I'm onto you.*

"Burnt them," she said. "Got them seen to."

"Did it hurt?" I asked, innocently.

"Not at all," she said. "Only took a few seconds."

Did it hang. Everyone knows burning means a red-hot poker that sizzles like bacon, and eats away through wart and finger and all till they drop off dead. That's what rat-faced Myra says, and her uncle is a dentist, and knows these things.

Gran leaned across the arm of the settee and dipped her hand into a bag of pandrops, considering her next move.

"You should get yours done." She nodded towards my finger, wrinkling her nose in disgust. The wart began to throb.

This was too much. Whose fault was it in the first place? Why should I suffer just because she'd had a lapse in personal hygiene?

I took my resolve in both hands. *You're not getting away with this.*

"I'm not getting burnt. You'll have to do something." I waved my disfigured finger accusingly in front of her nose.

She recoiled. Oh, I had her on the back foot all right.

"Me? What can I do?"

"Make it go away." I hissed, as fierce as I could without alerting my mother. *Get rid of it.*

She laughed.

"I can't do that, dear."

"Yes, you can." *And you will, oh yes.*

"And how's that, dear?"

I didn't intend to say it, but she stared at me with such a puzzled expression (*ha!*), without the slightest understanding (*ha!*), that I couldn't suppress it any longer. The word, lodged like a cork in my throat, erupted in a strangled shriek.

"Magic!" *There. It's out.*

The effect was immediate. She stiffened, her hand still buried in the bag of pandrops. She looked at me strangely, her lips pursed in a half-smile.

"Ah." She nodded, and popped a pandrop in each cheek, playing for time.

"Ah," I said. *Exactly.*

Then she bent and whispered to me close, her powdery breath tickling my ear.

"Magic, you reckon?"

"Yes." I said, firmly. *You heard.* She nodded, again, slowly. I'd got her, and she knew it.

She put her finger to her mouth in a shoosh, and looked round, checking carefully to the left, to the right and behind, where mum was pretending to fiddle with the traybake, while investigating cupboards on the sly.

"Only if you don't tell –" She jerked her head towards the kitchen.

"I promise," I whispered. *Not a word. Never ever.*

"Then I'll buy it off you."

It was an unexpected move. I didn't know there was a market for that sort of thing. But she'd obviously decided that, with her cover blown, there was no point in beating about the bush. A deal's a deal, after all. Presumably there were shops somewhere, or maybe a specialist trading floor full of sweaty city blokes barking out numbers in front of a jaggy green graph.

I frowned, trying to hide my confusion. She seized her chance.

"I'll give you 5op. The going rate. Best I can do."

Aloud, she added: "All right, dear, I'll come with you."

And even louder, for mum's benefit: "We're just away to the toilet."

There in the bathroom, under cover of the noise of flushing, we did our deal, Gran and I.

Wrapped Town

I pitched for a pound, on the grounds that I had two conjoined warts, and another on the way, plus they were unusually large examples. She said I was a chancer and knocked me down to 70p. Fair dos, though. I was happy, so was she; I with the money, she with the bargain. With the detached air of the true professional, she counted the coins into my hand, and snapped her purse shut and away into her pocket before I could blink.

On no account was mum to know. She wouldn't understand. She'd be livid, Gran said. Going on about daft stuff like that. Filling young heads. Wives' tales and nonsense. She tapped her nose conspiratorially – a generous, plump nose, so unlike the publicised kind.

"Agreed?"

"Yes," I whispered.

"Cross your heart?"

"And hope to die." I meant it.

She beckoned for my hand. I stretched it out, the soft, white knots of curdled skin throbbing at the rim of my nail. I wondered what she was going to do. I couldn't see any pots or potions – just the usual supermarket shampoos. She wasn't kitted out as dramatically as you'd want, in her cream blouse and faun skirt and earrings. But then, I reasoned, that was probably how she'd managed to get away with it for so long.

She gripped my finger tightly in one hand, and with the other hand she passed across it, slowly, not quite touching. I felt the hairs on my hand rise as a patch of coolness moved over it, like the feel of licked skin in the wind. Her head was bowed, her eyes fixed downways in tense concentration, so seriously that I scarce dared to breathe.

Finally, after a long, long minute, she relaxed and sat up straight, releasing my hand with a pat.

"There you go. All done."

Was that it? I examined my fingertip. The wart was still there, pulsing gently. I couldn't hide my disappointment. I'd expected it to fizzle away, or go up in smoke – anything at all, as long as it was spectacular.

She tapped her nose reassuringly.

"Don't you worry. It'll go as it came. Slow and steady. These things don't happen overnight."

It was my first piece of magic, though. Real, live stuff, shiver and shake stuff. Rat-faced Myra would be green. She'd never beat that with a whole streetful of dentists. I'd so enjoy telling her all about the puff of smoke and the flash of blue fire and the...

"Stop that!" A fierce slap landed and I squealed in pain. Gran glared.

"The more you play with it, the less it'll away. Leave it alone and be done with it."

Or else, said her eyes, louder than her mouth ever could.

For the first time, I was afraid of her. I'd never seen that expression before, her brows squeezed into tight wee skinfuls, her lips pressed in a thin, hard line. Yet in an instant, it was gone, and we returned to the living room, where mum sat waiting with a pot of stewed tea.

That night, back in my own bed, I wondered what would happen. My finger felt strange, right enough. The squashed knot beneath the plaster ached to a slow, dull beat all its own. Already, it felt different. It was hers now, not mine.

As I fell asleep, I saw it loosening itself, pulling up roots like a balloon about to sail, then detaching and flying off, a wee white rice krispy, out the window and off through the night across the roofs, over the hills and up to the heights with the sudden view of the sea, and all the way to North Berwick, tapping at Gran's kitchen window to be let in out of the cold. And she'd be waiting for it. She'd be waiting up, in her nighty at the window, feet freezing on the lino floor.

And she'd open the window and hold out her hand, and like the Blacky it would land, my white raisin, and push its hanging roots down deep into her finger, home and threaded in place where it belonged.

Would she let it stay? I wondered. Would she cover it with plaster? Would she sell it on?

I sank into sleep, exhausted.

It was still there, of course, in the morning. Still white, cracked, bleeding. Still holding on. But I forgot about it, eventually. I stopped peeling back the plasters, and they stayed in place for a whole day, or two or three, getting grubbier and rolling at the edges till they fell off by themselves.

One morning, when I was in the bath, the plaster floated away and there was nothing to see beneath. My skin was smooth and pink. When I scratched it with my nail, there was no bump or dot or roughness. The wart had gone.

It was a bright day, full of promise, with the whole weekend in front, and it was time to spend the 70p. I'd kept it in the pocket of my Sunday coat, where mum would never find it. I thought it best not to spend it till I'd kept my side of the deal. But that day, I went out and spent the lot, gorging on toffee chews and suffy dabs, the sour powder sucking my mouth dry till I couldn't swallow any more. I ended up spitting most of it into the gutter. I was happy. A clean, flat finger and a gobful of sugar.

Magic.

And if she died two weeks later, of a thing, mum said, that grew too big for the doctors to cut out, and choked her from the inside, like a cauliflower, mum said, spreading from place to place till she was more cauliflower than Gran and gave up, then it had nothing to do with me.

Bill McLaren Was My PE Teacher

T HERE'S ONLY ONE thing in life more humiliating than PE. I am about to do it. But this time, I'm going to do it my way.

And it's a magnificent pass there by Rutherford, beautifully creamed off the top there, and Rutherford almost up to the Scots 22, and that was a marvellous bit of running there by Rutherford –

Go away, Bill. This isn't the time. I'm a woman, now. Not a wee girl. I'm fourteen, after all.

The new red split seam frock is not too crushed, and I can almost stand on the heels of the £5.99 stilettos, bought in Dolcis' sale. I stuff my mum's lent turquoise nylon frock into a plastic bag – a cruel dress, with spaces for breasts I haven't got. I put it behind the bog among the Victorian stains and take a deep breath, my heart belting my ribs from inside, trying to make the tits I wish for nightly.

And Rutherford turns her back to take the impact and it's a huge kick by Morag Rutherford, well taken by Andy Irvine, out to Jim Aitken, back to Rutherford, and she's doing some great work out there on the edge of the mauls –

Not now, Bill. I'm thinking.

My black marker is running out, but there's room for one more message on the bog door. I started things weeks ago in the top right hand corner:

Robbie McHarg is beef.

Then, later, it appeared, in another desperate hand:

Too right he is 100% pure.

Then came a doorful of appreciative scrawls, until, down near the bottom:

Robbie fancies Shona C.

No! Everybody fancies Shona C, who has tits and long black hair. But next day I see:

Shona fancies Robbie.

Shit! So I write:

Shona C is an ugly cow.

I feel a lot better. That afternoon it gets personal:

Ya muckle slag.

I get to the point:

Tairt.

At four o'clock comes:

Shona C wants a fight with the lezzie bog bitch tomorrow 4 outside bog you will die!!!

Me and my marker have been silent for three days. For three days I've avoided that bog, and saved my pee for the science end. For three days, at four o'clock, Shona C, Mary Deans and the horrible, the hairy Shoog the Smoker have hung around the bogs like clouds of grey pre-prefect fug, and lusted for blood.

And now I write:

Robbie is mine.

There's no room for denials. The bog door is full. And tonight is the school Christmas dance.

Bill, Bill, where are you Bill?

Where were you, Bill, when we stood, arranged by chromosomes against the gym hall walls? Where were you when the picking happened, when I stood and prayed for salvation in the shape of a zitpocked youth who would lead me to the middle and away from the shame of the gym hall wall?

Games was bad enough, but this is no game, Bill. This is life, this is the big, bad world, and Robbie is mine in my dreams and country dancing is the battleground.

I pull my frock down over the black footless tights and shut the bog door behind me. But for the jockstrap, but for the gum shield, but for the bandage round my ears, I'm ready.

We've been practising Strip the Willow for the past four weeks. The humiliation of PE has been replaced by the humiliation of country dancing, in an effort to educate

Scottish youth in the habits that will save them the later humiliation of Scottish weddings.

But now, outside the bog door:

– Gie's a drag, eh?

– Haud oan, ya muckle tairt.

– Can ye see ma brastrap?

– That Zabby canna snog for toffee.

Shona, Shoog and Mary. I can smell the Charlie wafting under the door. There's nothing for it but to sit till they go. There's plenty other toilets.

The bang on the door echoes like the crack of the belt down the French end. The door judders and I put my hand up to save my knees.

– C'moan, you in there. There's folk waiting.

– Can ye no go in the other bog? I say.

Shoog's hairy red-nailed hand comes under the door and stabs a V in the direction of my ankles.

– You get ootta there this minute right or you're for it right?

Right. I take a deep breath, sort my frock and open the bog door. Shona is standing with her trademark blue marker. She pushes me outside. I need to play cool or I'm mince.

– Here! Somebody's been at it again.

I make for the door.

– Hoy! Speccy! Was that you?

I pretend not to hear.

– I'm talking to you, deef-lugs!

Wrapped Town

I'm gone.

And that's a beautiful bit of running there by Rutherford, out there on the wing, and a nifty piece of footwork as she crosses the Scots 22, out to Jim Renwick, to Milne, back to Rutherford –

I arrive in the gym hall, where the dancing is about to start. Charlie and Brut are fighting it out against a canopy of paper streamers. I stand against the wall and wait for the picking.

Whether it's rugby, hockey, Strip the Willow or snogs, it's always the same. Out strut the alphas. They graze the assembled pack with an experienced eye: the form, the turf, the training. You, you, you and you. And me? What about me?

The dust clears and the floor heaves and I am left facing Skinny Deekie, who will snake his finger round my back to my chest and be disappointed. A chord, a bow, a whistle, and we're off. The Military Two-Step ground-kicks around the hall and my shins sting mightily.

Robbie McHarg is 100% beef. He weaves in black denim through the throng and is magnificent – the nearest thing Hawick High has ever had to Eddie Kidd. Shona, Shoog and Mary are picked up by the boys at the back of the English class and are steering them expertly around the hall. Shona glares at me as we pass and I waltz Deekie swiftly into a dark corner and twist his sticky mouth from my neck.

My future happiness hinges on the Ladies' Choice.

I used to read *The Jackie.* How innocent, how tame that world seems now, as I stand sweating over the small print of my future.

Dear Jackie, I have acne. Dear Jackie, I'm in love with the French assistant. Dear Jackie, my parents won't let me out after ten.

Dear Jackie, I am about to begin the Ladies' Choice.

We arrange ourselves XY-XX against the gym hall wall, in slow-motion silence.

Dear Jackie, what if I can't run fast enough?

Brut-and-Charlie steam rises and damps the paper streamers.

Dear Jackie, what if he says no?

Shona paws the ground with her stilettos and snorts. Shoog flexes her nicotine fingers. Robbie is sweetly oblivious against the gym hall wall. He gazes into the middle distance, like Eddie Kidd across a row of London buses.

Dear Jackie, what if

    – Take your partners –

        Shona tenses.

            Ground-stick –

Dear Jackie, what

    – for the La –

        Shona up on her heels.

            Ground-stick –

Dear Jackie

    – d –

        Shona leans.

            Ground-stick –

Dear God

    – ies Cho –

        Shona creaks.

            the B – B – Ba –

Dear

        Dear

                Dear

SHOOM! I am off.

And it's a magnificent piece of footwork there by Morag Rutherford, just pipping the edge there from Shona Cranston with a lovely little swivel of the hips. And it's Shoog McGeechan with a shimmy there and a touch of the old size 18s to the shins and can Rutherford hold her off? By Jove she certainly can and she sails over the boys' 22 but Cranston and McGeechan are right on her tail and she's almost over the line and there's Robbie McHarg waiting in touch as 30 stones of Scotland's finest bear down on him –

Shut up, Bill. I am holding Robbie's hand.

I am holding Robbie's hand in a fingerlock and whisking him onto the dance floor. And Shona, Shoog and Mary are staring at a faint cloud of Brut.

Robbie looks dazed but he's not going anywhere but into the field with me. I am too busy gazing up into his Eddie Kidd eyes to see that the lineout has formed and I'm up there in a set with Shona, Shoog and Mary and the boys from the back of the English class.

Strip the Willow is the toughest game in the repertoire. Teeth have been lost, bones shattered, shins bloodied and grown men brought to their knees, and that's just the first eight bars. I hitch my frock up with one hand, clinging tightly to Robbie with the other, and as the music starts I am preparing for the fight of my life.

And they're off, Rutherford and McHarg, the ham and eggs of Scottish country dancing, with a tight birl down the middle of the field and it's a magnificent sight, this pair –

Behind Robbie there's a blur of faces as Shona-Shoog-Mary-Shona-Shoog-Mary birl past his shoulder. His hands are warm and firm. And the moment's all too brief, for I have to let them go and pass him down the spinning line.

And Rutherford slips out to clear the way for McHarg, and he's well taken by Shona Cranston, out to big McGeechan, out to Deans, back to Cranston, and she's holding on there for dear life as she tanks her way through the wall of bodies, and McHarg is way back down at the end of the lineout, taking quite a knock there –

Robbie is whirling blindly down the bottom end with Shona as Shoog comes in for the tackle, hisses 'lezzie' in my ear and heaves me across into the next scrum. I get up with Deekie's Pringle spiked on my heel. He leers and slides his hand up my leg and I jab an illegal elbow at his jockstrap.

And it's back out to Deans, a flip over to McGeechan, to Cranston, McGeechan, back to Cranston, and just look at the smooth teamwork there, and Shona Cranston has possession and there's no way she's being parted from McHarg –

Robbie lands back at the top with Shona still attached to his jeans belt and trying to slot into my space in the set. But he whisks round deftly and she loses her grip and I'm able to nip back in there and throw him a grin. To my amazement, to my joy, to my eternal glorious heavenly rapture, he grins back with those dark Eddie Kidd eyes, and angels chime in above the accordions.

Shona, Shoog and Mary clench jaws as they make short work of the boys from the back of the English class and play passes down the line. Eventually it's my turn and, my eyes fixed on Robbie, I advance into the middle for the birl. We spin and spin, and I can't let go, and would've spun on happily up to the angels, if something hadn't fallen out of my pocket.

I look down to see my black marker rolling across the floor to Shona's feet. She picks it up and narrows her brow like a propforward who's just taken a size 18 in the jockstrap and is keen to exact revenge.

Off I go down the line, weaving among the boys from the back of the English class, and each time blissfully back to Robbie.

It's when I get to the bottom that I go flying into touch.

Let's see that again.

Rutherford is flying down the middle there, look at her go, and yes, there's that foot coming out, it's McGeechan with a fly bit of obstruction, and surely that has to be a penalty –

But there's no time for protest cos there's an elbow in my eye and a strappy sandal gouging a hole in my shin down under 30 stones of 3M's finest.

– Hands off, speccy.

– He's mine ya lezzie bitch right?

I'm in no position to argue. I lie on the floor, waiting for my inevitable demise, and hear the angels clearing their throats for a requiem.

But what's this? The bodies are heaved aside and my eyes pull into painful focus on a pair of Eddie Kidd peepers just inches from my face. Robbie – Robbie McHarg! – reaches out and touches my leg. I've a gaping ladder right down to the footless foot of my tights, and a dribble of blood is making its way down my ankle.

And then he speaks, this dark-eyed motorbike god, as I lie in heaven with his hand on my leg.

Three little words that mean the world. Three little words that I'll keep and cherish till the end of time.

Wrapped Town

– Come off it.

Shona, Shoog and Mary shrink back on their bloodstained stilettos.

Thank you, Robbie McHarg. Thank you for noticing my pain. Thank you for defending my corner. The angels are singing the Old Spice ad and my heart thumps big proud bazoobas right out across the gym.

*

It's late, Bill, and I'm on my way home from the school Christmas dance, my ears still ringing and my shin still stinging. What a game, what a day, what a country!

And that was a magnificent finish there by Rutherford, the girl of the match here at Murrayfield today, winning her first cap for the Scottish side and there'll no doubt be many, many more. And I can tell you they'll be dancing in the streets of Hawick tonight –

I'm dancing, Bill. I'm dancing all the way along Buccleuch Street and up the Loan.

Quite the Thing

MY DAD SAYS I'll maybe have to do pictures. I've never done that afore but I've seen it on the telly. They've got eyes and faces for everybody in the whole world. That's why I've got to do the man.

You can see oor bit gy well from up the hill, seen it's white and fair stands oot from the others cos it's painted. You can see the back bedroom window and work oot where the slanty attic one is with the no curtains behind the Hoggs' bit. If Jane's coming to oor bit I go into the back bedroom so I can see her come oot the front door, miles away, this wee walking dot, and I ken it's her, though. That road I ken to get ready. And I kent she was coming, cos we'd phoned aboot it.

I could do the pictures first, maybe. If you want. While I remember. You could do dad or mum even or onybody or maybe me. Have you got bits for me in there? Eyes and that? When did you get them?

Wrapped Town

Where we were was at the tyre. It's a good tyre, up by the cemetery, up the back brae, and you can get a good scary swing. You can birl ana, sideyways, cos it's just the one rope, and you can get somebody to birl you and birl you till the rope's tight, and then you can birl back the way, with the sun getting in your eyes, roond and roond till you get dizzy and maybe a wee bit sick from screaming. But it's no scary. The best thing is to stand up and put your heid back and look up at the tree, but Ali can only sit as she's five.

We found a den in the gorse bushes. You can tell it's a den cos there's sherbet dab tubes on the ground, and matches, but we didna play with matches. You're meant to strike them away from you so you dinna get burnt. I've never seen onybody there but they must come and go cos of the sherbet dab tubes. They must be on their holidays ana.

In the books in the holidays they have ginger beer. It's aye lashings and tastes magic and cold and there's this dog and boats. I dinna think we're allowed it cos it's beer but they're English. My dad has beer locked in a cupboard under the table he made. It's formica and he made it in the shed.

We sometimes get lemonade, but it's dear. Once my cousin came and wanted diluting orange in his lemonade, but my mum goes, either or. That's the Kelso ones.

Jane had a tube of Smarties so we divided them into colours and ate them. She goes, dinna eat them all at once, like my mum, but we did. There was blue ones in the picture but you never get ony in the tube.

Onyroad, this man came up the hill. He was bigger than a dot because we could see he had a jaiket ower his shooder, holding it with his finger. I canna mind what colour. Maybe broon. I suppose it was kinna funny to be oot for a walk cos it wasna Sunday and there was no hooses up the hill. But onyroad it was Jane's go so I lifted oot Ali and Jane sat in the tyre and cawed and I pushed.

My dad does a thing where he pushes you till it's high enough to run right under the swing and then you go really high. Sometimes I get scared that I'll go right roond the top and fall, but my dad says you'd stay put cos of the force, but I dinna believe him. The rope is straight like a kinna stick holding you doon, but when you get to the top it'll fall like wool and that'll be you.

So this man gets nearer. Jane goes, maybe he's got lost? I go, must be gy donnert as all the shops and that are doon the hill. He gets up to us and looks fair serious and goes, what's the time? and it's a quarter past three. Then he goes, have you seen a wee white dog, and we go, no and we think he must have lost it, and then he can't be that bothered cos he goes, do you want a push? Then Jane starts kinna giggling and I look and then I pretend I didna look cos he's got his thing hinging oot.

Wrapped Town

I ken I shouldna have giggled but I couldna help it. He was pushing Jane on the swing and his thing was hinging oot and he hadna even noticed. He must have walked all the way up the hill, maybe even along the street and that, quite the thing, and folk looking. I didna fair look, though.

When you do the pictures and that, can you do, like, all bits? Just the faces? I suppose it would be difficult to get the pictures for, ken.

He was gy tall, as tall as my dad, and maybe aboot the same age. You'd think he'd notice, but then I suppose it's gy easy to forget. You often forget to do your zip and then it's dead embarrassing when you've been to the toilet. Not at school, mind, cos we're no allowed troosers at school.

And he was smiling and quite the thing. Ali didna ken what I was giggling for but she was giggling ana. She does that. He pushed Jane really high, and I suppose it was gy scary, but you couldna tell cos she was just hinging on and laughing and cawing and being quite the thing. And maybe we thought we'd get a shot ana, with him pushing.

But this went on for a while with him pushing, and we didna ken what to do except hing aboot, so in the finish we ran doon the hill. Or maybe I ran doon the hill and Ali came with me. I didna really leave Jane because she was on the swing and onyroad there was noplace else to go so we knew where she was. We ran down to the den and waited. Me and Ali.

We were in the den and we ducked doon and I go, did you see that? But Ali didna ken what I was on aboot and I wasna going to let her go and get a look. Onyroad she's only five.

You canna go on the tyre after it's been raining. Least you can, but it's got water in it and leaves and you have to lift it up and cowp it oot but you have to be careful or you'll get soaked. I got soaked once. You have pull up the tyre right up by the bottom and then leave go and then it falls and kicks kinna jaggedy like and the water comes oot. It's gy heavy, mind.

So after a bit we're waiting doon in the gorse bushes and wondering what to do. We canna get Jane cos she's up on the swing and we canna get her doon and onyroad it takes a while for the tyre to stop. Like when you try to jump off at the real swings, you have to wait until it feels right or you'll just do your knees in. Like when you get wee stanes and muck all stuck in your hands from falling and it's sore. I had a teesh scurl there once.

He had on kinna broon clothes or navy, and troosers and this jaiket on his shooder. I canna mind what he did with the jaiket when he was pushing. I canna mind the troosers. I didna fair like to look. I was looking at his face cos it was the only place you could look. He had big eyes and they were dark and he was kinna bald and he didn't have wee eyes, no, they were big. Like those cartoon ones you draw with a circle and a

line through the middle for the eyelids. Like Deppety Dawg,
Aye. Like those. And the hair. Less. More in the middle, like
a V. Like that. Dark.

That's great. That's just like.

My grandad's bald. I asked him once how he didna have
hair, though he used to look like Clark Gable in the photos,
and they all laughed, my mum and dad and everybody. And
he goes, an accident. And he goes, something hit my heid.
They all laughed again and I was fair vexed for him because
it isna that funny, something bashing your heid and losing all
your hair, like a roof and that, like the trapdoor in the attic
because I saw that once and it looked fair sore.

It's like, I'm forever growing oot of things and my mum is
aye at me with the scissors and you'd think folk could grow
their hair back, especially as he's a hairdresser. It must have
been a gy big accident but they dinna talk aboot it. We have
chips there when we go to Kelso, from the place next door.
And we have sandwiches to put them in but she puts on
ower much butter and you have to bite it with your teeth like
cheese.

Ali and me are doon in the bushes and we're wondering
what to do, but we dinna want to go back up cos he was
pushing gy hard. And we dinna stick wir heids up because
we're still giggling. But then Jane comes doon, quite the
thing, and goes, maybe we should get back. I go, is he away?

and she goes, uh-uh, and I go, was that no scary? cos it was gy high, and she goes, no. She's older than me.

We wait in the den for a bit and when we look oot he's away. But Jane's fair tane with hersel cos she got a push off him and she goes, you shouldna have giggled. And we go home.

It's the next day and I'm still giggling at the man who didna even notice about his thing, so mum goes simmer doon, I'll give you something to giggle at. I'm crying but I canna tell her because of Jane and her mum who'll kill her, but in the end I do tell her though I canna remember how cos I dinna say 'thing'. It comes oot aboot the man and she phones Margaret and then dad and he phones the police and Jane's no gonna speak to me cos we'd said no to tell. Jane's mum Margaret goes, I know nothing aboot it and Jane gets asked and you can tell she's no gonna be my best friend ony mair after that.

No, he didna touch us, cos we ran away to the gorse bushes and you have to ask Jane about the rest. He was tall and thin with Deppety Dawg eyes with a line through for eyelids. Hair like a baldy V.

I seen him again after that. He walks by us gy ner every day on the way to school but he doesna look at us. You'd have to come wi us and I'd show you. There's this new girl came, he's a pal of her dad's and comes aboot the hoose. I telt her but she didna believe me.

You see if you get new people, who're just born, how do you get their eyes and that? Or maybe you just use their parents' eyes, if they're the same?

That's the best mooth. I'm no sure if it's his. Maybe somebody else's. But I canna fair mind the mooth. But that's his eyes. Definitely.

Jane got a clouting off her mum. She's still no speaking and she's got my Action Girl. You say to your mum, dinna tell, and what's the first thing they do? And she goes, tell me, tell me, if anything like that happens again. And she looks at me fair hard and goes, now you will, won't you? and I go, yes, with my teeth shut and looking at her hard ana.

But I dinna ken if I would. You can get into the awfest lot of trouble.

Holiday Home

WE CAME BACK home after a fortnight away on holiday in Whitley Bay. Even though we'd not been far – not much over fifty miles, in fact – the house looked entirely different on our return.

We noticed the effect as soon as we entered the hall. The colours had changed, for a start. The carpet was brighter than before. The living room suite was a zingier shade of burgundy. The objects on the sideboard – the photos, the trophies, the faux-stone water feature – were drawing attention to themselves in an unaccustomed, startling way. The kitchen sparkled; even the grimy mosaic-patterned lino gleamed like a walkway of small gems.

It was as if someone had fiddled with the colour and contrast knobs in every room of the house. Everything, from the dust on the upstairs banister to the scuffmarks on the downstairs skirting, had suddenly come alive.

Wrapped Town

We couldn't put our finger on it for a while. We were disappointed when everything returned to its normal dullness after a couple of days. Then we realised, quite suddenly, that the dullness was us.

Our fortnight away had given the house the chance to wake up, restore its batteries, recover its vim, and live a little. Separated from our dreary predictability and boring routines, it had experienced something of a liberation. In other words, it had had a holiday, too.

We decided to go away more often after that. We didn't like to cramp its style.

Jules Horne

Reinventing the Beach

The Home Beach was invented by Croatian surgeon Aleksandar Stošić. It was designed for orthopaedic and therapeutic use in hospitals, fitness centres and the home.

O NCE UPON A time there was a beach. It was a beach covered in stones, not sand. The stones were round and smoothed by the action of water and time. One day, after more water and more time, they would become sand, but not for the duration of this story.

A man walked across the beach. If it had been a beach covered in sand, not stones, he'd have been swinging his arms, curling his toes into the soft grit, enjoying the slight sinking and shifting below him.

It wasn't. His trousers rolled up, he was hirpling across the stones in something close to agony. Though round and smooth, they were large stones. However, they were not large enough to accommodate a whole foot, nor even just its heel or ball. They were roughly the size of eggs, ranging from duck or swan size all the way down to bantam. He might as well have been walking on eggs, in fact, given his slow and painful progress.

Each stone ground deep into the soles and arches of his foot, until his weight was borne by the best match between skin and stone, stone and skin.

Finding the right spot to place his foot was a matter of care and bravado. At first, he tried to seek out suitable stones, test them for stability, rest his foot on top then gradually increase the pressure. It seemed the most sensible way to proceed. But as his balance shifted, and the proportion of the body borne on the back foot began to equal the proportion carried on the front, and arrive at the critical point where his weight would transfer from one to the other, the stones moved.

They were not fixed. They were rolling stones, and although there was no tilt or seismic upheaval below them to keep them in motion at this time, they were capable of rolling under pressure from above. Under the man's foot, they slid against each other, grinding away a small surface each from the other, and found a new arrangement where friction kept them tight together, balanced point to point, with his weight above to keep them steady. Unfortunately, this had the effect of sending painful edges into places the man wasn't expecting. These were usually the underside of his arches – the softest, most vulnerable part of his body, the oyster-soft smooth and ticklish parts of him, which were all the more surprising for being right next to the hard, horny leather of his heels.

Carefully picking his way across the stones was not the way to go. They weren't cooperating. He decided just to give himself up to their random action. Since they were moving in any case, it didn't make any difference where he landed. He would stare straight ahead, making no pretence at selectiveness. He would keep his eyes on the line where the sea met the sky, both now turning a tender shade of orange. The stones would do whatever they wanted down below, and he would keep his legs moving, one then the other, and let his feet find something to land on.

This seemed to work better. By walking faster, each foot had less time to dwell on the stone, and thus the pain. As quick as they landed, they lifted again, giving the pebbles less opportunity to grind into the parts that yielded most.

He was reminded of hot coals. It was a question of will and timing, he'd heard. First, you needed to be psyched up to the point where the entirely valid objections of your rational mind were overruled. That was achieved by talking to other people who'd already danced the coal-walk and lived. "It's fun," they'd lie. "It's exhilarating" and "it's like nothing else," they'd add, more truthfully, followed by "speed is of the essence."

For people didn't walk across hot coals. They didn't stroll or saunter. They ran. They sprinted. They hared as fast as their legs could carry them. Like hell, like the blazes, like all the fast, fiery similes rolled into one.

His face squeezed into a range of grimaces as he walked the stones. Sometimes his eyes shut tight, and his mouth along with it. Sometimes his eyes stretched wide open, and his mouth followed suit. Sometimes one did one and one the other, with no attempt at coordination.

He didn't bother to hide these comic expressions. No one was watching, and he needed all his concentration for the job in hand.

His arches weren't worthy of the name. They were flat as roads. They spanned nothing taller than a hair, and even a hair would have been crushed ovoid below them. They had fallen. If they had fallen any further, they would have dropped below the horizon.

There were advantages. For one thing, he had managed to avoid military service. For another – but there wasn't another. There were only drawbacks. All sorts of careers were ruled out. Ballet, police, guardsman, of course. But others, too, less obvious: security guard, shop assistant, salesman, customs officer. Anything that involved the least amount of walking about, the least standing upright, whether at a counter, desk or entrance gate. He couldn't be a dog-walker or an usherette. He'd be no good whatsoever as an athlete or burglar, with all the running involved.

It was getting easier to walk across the beach. The cycling of his legs seemed to have made him lighter on the stones, and the pain was no longer so great. He was able to devote less thought to his feet, and more to his face, which was aching, too, from the unaccustomed stretching and clenching.

He kept his gaze on the horizon, by now an angry orange, like the heart of a fire. He kept walking.

He was reminded of a story he'd once heard, of a mermaid who traded her tail for legs that felt like knives to walk on. It always seemed like an unfair transaction to him. He could fully understand the reaction of her merfellows, who put her over the equivalents of their knees and told her not to be so silly, that no love was worth distorting yourself for and that she could change herself to suit the prince as much as she liked, she'd still fall short of the mark. It was a consummate, modern lesson, just as applicable to breasts, weight and nose jobs as to tails.

Treading across the stones, he wondered nonetheless about her courage. How had she kept her mind off the knives? Were knives really that painful at all? He'd cut himself deeply, once. It hadn't hurt in the slightest, as far as he could recall. Not for several minutes. His finger had bled profusely and needed several stitches. He hadn't felt a thing until it started to heal, until the wound stopped being fresh and supple, and started being stiff, and hardening at the cut edges. He remembered only the insistent throb of his slit finger, as if the muffled underground workings of his body were now exposed to the daylight. It had been like opening the bonnet of a car with its engine running. The blood had squirted into his handkerchief. He had found it interesting, not sore.

So maybe the knife-walking was something you got used to, like a permanent headache, and maybe your mind found ways to deal with it. Such as looking outside yourself and your bothers. Such as keeping your eye on the ball.

The sun was dissolving into the sea. It made a kind light. His hands looked golden. His fingertips were haloed with backlight. He could taste the brine on his lips. His hair was thick and strawy with salt.

He didn't look at his feet. They were apart from him now, someone else's feet. They felt very far away. He was vaguely aware of them taking steps, moving him forward mechanically. The ground was gently sloping away beneath him. He must be almost at the water.

The shock of the wet hit him. It was cold and delicious. He felt the foam massage his toes with the gentlest touch and fall away. Seafoam. What the mermaid had become when she'd given up on her impossible love and returned home, ghostly tail between her grafted legs. He wondered whether she'd had a memory of that tail when she walked. Did she have not only the knives to contend with, but also the phantom itches and swishes of her amputated fish-part? Had she missed the things she could no longer do? The feel of a powerful kick that surged her forward, hair rippling behind? The tickle of fish in her slipstream? Had she flexed her old ghost muscles against the disappointing emptiness of air?

He stood and let them bathe, the numb feet. They chilled into feeling. They were sore. His soft mollusc arches ached and burned. He wouldn't have been surprised to see a hiss of steam rise from them. Deliberately, he'd tricked himself into walking all the way to the water's edge, so that now, he'd have to walk all the way back. His shoes lay together next to the road, back where he'd parked the car. The socks were stuffed inside them. The only way back was across the pebbles. He'd forced himself to do twice as much walking as he really could.

He would rest. Sit down and watch the melt of the light. He'd earned it. Lowering himself onto the beach, he rested his hands behind him and winced as the stones stabbed his palms and then his backside. The hot-coal dance again. He had to shift, shift, shift from one point of pressure to the other. There was nowhere for respite. Even the startling chromatography of the sky couldn't keep his mind off his predicament.

A dog appeared, a long, bony lurcher, bounding easily over the pebbles. Some way off walked a woman in boots, a length of lead dangling from her hand. A few feet away from the man, the dog stopped and sniffed its way forward. He wasn't sure about dogs. There were good ones and mean ones.

It nuzzled around behind him. It was interested in his pocket. He twisted out of its way, putting his hand out to push its wet nose from his jacket. As he did so, his weight ground harder into fewer stones and, trying to avoid the pain, he lost balance and toppled backwards.

His head just missed the stones. He curved his spine and felt the hard points dig into every bone of it. There was nothing for it but to give in, to fall right back onto the pebble bed and lie there. He felt surprisingly comfortable, spreadeagled across the beach in his thick coat. The dog's muzzle poked into his face and slobbered his chin. He spluttered it away and started to laugh. To giggle, even. His belly let out all its hoarded tension and heaved in great, shaking gasps, each one jabbing him again and again into the stones. He crooked his knees up and splashed his flat feet in the rising water, one after the other, treading the stones as if they were grapes, giggling like a schoolchild.

There was still the long way back to the car. He looked up at the darkened sky. The first star was out. Venus, maybe. The one that appeared before the others, before the sun had even had time to drop out of sight.

He wanted to take the beach home with him. Plant it in his living room. Carpet the house with it. Paint the walls the colours of the sky.

It was good for him, the beach-walking. It was good for his feet. It was medicinal. Each step made his feet stronger, harder. The muscles tensed and toughened. The arches remembered what they might have been and strained at least in the right direction.

He would, then. He'd take the beach home. Learn to live with it. He'd lay it out on the floor and walk across it every day. Wake up to it in the morning and lower his feet onto basalt, not the thick, white rug that purred by his bedside. Stumble across it to the bathroom. Stand on it in front of the toilet, shifting his weight from left to right, heel to ball, as he waited for his bladder to empty. In the kitchen, in the living room, and up and down the corridor, walking and wearing the stones, feeling them shift under him as nothing ever did in the clean, concrete world he lived in.

Or maybe just a corner of beach. A boxed beach. A square of it, a metre each side. He'd keep it in his bedroom, under the bed behind the white, purring rug, and he'd pull it out every morning and stand on it and tread the stones as though they were grapes, and remember the taste of salt and the colour of the sky, while his arches strained from the knives.

Radar Bird

So THIS IS the pitch, right? It'll be a stonker. Believe it. Right from the opening credits, popcorn will sit unscoffed, Coke unsooked, sweetie wrappers unrustled. One-film stands in the back row will remain unsnogged.

Women will laugh, men cry, couples argue and break up and make up and make love, and maybe live just a wee bit better for having seen it.

When they go out into the night to the trams and the tubes and the car parks, chips will be the last thing on their minds. They'll walk through the dark with an empty soreness inside for all the loves they killed and lost. But deeply, bittersweetly happy.

Playing she: let's go for Juliette Binoche – sweet, mysterious, passionate, vulnerable. Outfits by Ghost. Simple, effortless, with a touch of whimsy.

Playing he: how about Michael Douglas? Grim-chinned, baby-eyed, a veneer of dimpled innocence masking innards of the purest evil. Costumes by someone stiff and square-shouldered and very Eighties. Possibly Next. He's the baddie, right?

The basic plot is girl-meets-guy, girl-loses-guy. There isn't a happy ending, a froth of white and invitations, unless you count the fact that she had a narrow escape from a life of unspeakable misery. Which is something to be grateful for, though not fantastic box office.

But the first bit, the meeting bit, the strings-and-roses bit, doesn't count. It's just the prequel. It's a prequel that will never be made, since the main feature recasts the past and blights all previous mirth. Hindsight. That old killer of unravelled joy.

So let's ditch the prequel. Let's cut to the chase. What we've got in front of us is that classic favourite, girl-loses-guy.

There are two problems with this scenario, you say:

Problem one: It sounds careless. What did she do? Drop him at the checkout? Chuck him in the bucket with the tattie peelings?

The truth is, she wasn't careless at all. She cared a lot, and did her best to show it, often, with all the affection she could reasonably spare.

Problem two: It sounds as if she played an active part in what happened. Sadly, she didn't. It would be more accurate to say that she was lost.

Wrapped Town

Lost? Where? In the woods, you say? Did she mislay her trail of breadcrumbs? Drop her compass? Or was she lost metaphorically, in a vague, mind-body-spirit sort of way? You're right. Let's have facts. Let's have stats. The truth is, she was losed.

Ah, the passive. It won't go away, will it? You're right. She isn't the agent at all. He is. Let's turn them round again. Him then her. That order. And find a verb. Yes, all the euphemisms in the world don't make it any easier. Dump. Ditch. Discard. Chuck. Abandon.

So here's where we're at. Guy-dumps-girl. This is a hump-and-dump film. A fuck-and-chuck, if you'll pardon. A new genre.

So. Over the opening credits we see her at the airport, waiting anxiously at the head of a long queue as he comes haring up, case in hand, tie and jacket flapping. City guy. Busy busy. Perfunctory peck and apologies.

Cut to plane interior. He is loosening his tie and wriggling irritably. She is looking out the window, crying.

Why is she crying? Because she doesn't understand. For weeks, she's been doing everything wrong. Flashback: chopping onions, booking holidays, folding clothes, choosing shoes. The wrong shoes, for chrissake. She can't even choose her own shoes properly. She's cracked it to a T, the art of reliably and flawlessly doing everything wrong. Which is odd, because before that, she'd been doing everything more or less right.

On with the dialogue:

HE: What's wrong?

SHE: Nothing.

She continues looking out of the window, crying, but in an aesthetically pleasing way that doesn't smudge her makeup.

You're right to raise the issue of cliché. Much appreciated. That exchange crops up in pretty well every film about relationships ever shot. Though often, if you'll forgive, with different personnel:

SHE: What's wrong?

HE: Nothing.

Or

PARENT: What's wrong?

CHILD: Nothing.

Or

HUMAN: What's wrong?

ANDROID: Nothing.

But yes, it's always the same general subtext:

HE: Everything, but don't imagine for one instant that I'm going to talk to you about it. It's such a painful can of worms that I don't know where to start. You're distant, I'm depressed, we're not communicating, we've stopped loving, it's all crumbling slowly about our ears and we're afraid to press too much in case it collapses. And there's no point in starting a scene right now cos if we're going to embark on a row it will have to be the mother of all rows and that's a thing I'm putting off as long as possible. Now bugger off and leave me alone.

So you see, it's the best available line in the circumstances. Crisp, short, economical. But we can look at the alternative. The truth.

HE: What's wrong?

SHE: Everything.

HE: For God's sake, don't start. Cos if you're gonna start, I'm getting off this plane right now. I'm not spending a week with you snivelling on like a tragedy queen. Jesus, we're on holiday. Blow your nose, there's people looking –

CUT! See? It's not attractive. Not filmic.

They arrive at the main location. The setting is a Greek island, generically blue (sky) and blue (sea) sandwiching a paradise of heat and beaches. Montage: taxi, bare white hotel room, stripping off the thick layers of London. She puts on a long yellow dress, he wears unlikely British shorts. They collapse separately onto the separate beds and look at the ceiling. He cracks open a bottle of beer.

How much time do you have? Ah. Yes, let's cut to the chase. Not that there's a chase as such. After all, it's an island. No room. And too expensive. Always an eye on production costs.

Anyway, the key scene, the scene it all revolves around, is this:

Guy-tells-girl-he-has-found-someone-else.

This concept is first introduced with a scrap of dialogue. Setting: outside the restaurant, in the twinkling dark, after the first meal out, the first bottle of wine, the first unwinding:

HE: It's not that I don't love you.

SHE: ???

The ??? can be expressed in various ways, depending on the skill of the actress. Eyebrows, mouth, the horizontal lines across the brow – all can be used to great effect. It's a gift, really. A chance to show a wide emotional range of huge complexity.

For him, too. Yes, it's a great line. An awful line, too. Great in its awfulness, both grammatical and emotional. Two negatives, for a start. 'Not' and 'don't'. You can be forgiven for thinking they make a plus. That they cancel each other out. That he loves her. That would be a mistake. The same mistake she makes, in fact.

What a line! Is it an apology? A confession? A reassurance?

What is he saying in that moment? It's clear the words didn't come about by chance. Such crushing banality can only be achieved with an unusual effort of thought, precision and practice.

The full subtext would take at least half an hour to express:

HE: It's over but I'm too much of a coward to tell you straight. Look into my eyes and read them. It's all in there. The message has been there for weeks, big and clear. Why won't you read it? Why are you so obtuse? Don't make me say things directly. I don't know how. I have the words but they hurt in my mouth. They're sharp and bitter and ugly and don't suit me. Don't force me. I want *you* to say them. I want *you* to take the initiative. Why do you think I've been treating you like that? Criticising, nit-picking, niggling? I want you to hate me. Then you'll say the words that I can't. Believe me, it'll be easier. Oh, and there's someone else.

She doesn't crack the code. Her ??? is a genuine ???. She isn't feigning incomprehension to gain time.

He thinks he's said something meaningful. He thinks he's told it like it is. He thinks he's been big, bold and incisive. He's feeling relieved, therefore. That it's all out in the open. That she knows.

In fact, she knows sweet shit. That's why she says ??? And when he starts crying, from relief and possibly the strain of thinking up such an immortal line, she says ??? again, and gives him a comforting hug. Therethere. A warm old motherhug for the little lost boy. You're all right. It's OK. Therethere. I understand. Shhhhh. It's OK. Ad lib ad inf.

How can she be so selfish, you ask? Is she doing it deliberately? Pretending not to understand? Forcing him to say the ugly words? Is she entirely incapable of subtlety? Of imagination? Of compassion? Self, self, self, always self. And here he is, trying so hard to be kind. As illustrated by:

HE: I'm sorry.

Oh dear, you say. That old chestnut. That catch-all cover-the-cracks. That handy self-absolution.

Stay with it. It's a challenge, especially for Michael Douglas. Here's what lies beneath.

HE: I'm sorry that you exist. That you were born. That you can't be unmade. That you can't be deleted by simply shutting my eyes. And, particularly, that you have a toothbrush in the glass by my sink. And I apologise for all the painful things I've ever done to you, and, while I'm at it, for all the painful things I'm about to do, especially in the very near future. Beginning in just a few moments. Beginning now.

You see? Much more to it than meets the eye.

You're getting impatient. That's great. You want to see how it ends. You're hooked. Stay with it.

The point is, love stops. There's nothing you can do. It's not intrinsically a problem. A love that's puttered to a halt without a fuel stop in nearby reach is not necessarily in trouble. You can get out, relax, take a breather, enjoy the view. It might be a pleasant view, you never know. Peaceful. Familiar. Comfortable.

The problem isn't usually the stopping of an old love. You can live with that. People do, by and large. No, it's the starting of a new one. A huge, red, shiny sports job zooming into the layby, headlights flashing, horn beeping, offering you a lift somewhere. Somewhere new. So you're going places. Not stranded on the verge.

It's a metaphor. It doesn't have to be a real car.

And when that new love zooms off into the sunset, or the new dawn, or whatever looks most scenic, what we're left with is a great big hole. A gap in the story.

You want to follow the new car? Shame. That's so obvious. This is not about obvious. The new love is probably pretty much like any other: soaring hyperbole for the first few weeks, or even months if they're lucky, then flattening out in time, till you'd be hard pushed to call it a hummock.

And the ending? Not pretty. Malaria, perhaps. Or bourgeois boredom. Or even bridge. The day they find themselves playing bridge – oh, dear, that will be a day to look in the mirror and weep. And death, of course, ultimately. That goes almost without saying.

But that's way off the track. This isn't about the new car, if you'll forgive.

Have you time? Just a minute? Then let's cut back to where she's still standing, having uttered her ???, and offered her therethere hug, and having heard his "I'm sorry" mumbled tearfully into the shoulder of her long yellow dress.

Wait! Hear me out! Let's cut to after he's said the ugly truthful words and magically, in a moment, transformed his guilt into her nausea, and a rushing in the ears, and a protective disbelief all in one.

Or cut to the swim? Yes, let's cut to an island shore. Albania is out there somewhere. Warships sailing, grey distant silhouettes up and down the Ionian Sea, if that's technically possible. Small sailboats dotted about, maybe. A deepening sunset.

Don't go! Nearly there! Into the water she slips, from a barnacled rock. Into the picture-blue water bloodied by the sun. A shock of awakening. A numbness cleansed. It's a dreamlike place. Down goes her head, below the water, where there's only her and deafness and her heartbeat and her bursting lungs.

Wait! Listen! Up above, somewhere in a tree, a bird sings. It sounds like a radar, softly pipping across the water.

This is what it sings:

You see? The bird song, pipping in the almost dark.

And the crickets. A rhythm section, if you like.

This is what the crickets do:

Can you hear it?

And the engine, away in the distance, a moped changing gear:

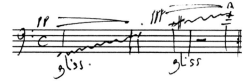

Off into the dark, fading till it's gone.

The Beating of Bread

OH! THE BEATING of bread! She was at it again, kneading and pounding and mashing and mauling the dough, slapping it heavily on the table, knocking it back, flattening any bubbles of life that were so cocky as to make their appearance inside it.

Her husband wondered, sometimes, as he shuffled his evening paper next door.

He'd hear the squeak of the stool as she pushed it next to the high shelves. He'd hear the creak of her hips as she stepped her large weight up onto it. He'd hear the humph of her breath as she strained her arms to the scales, and the clatter of the loose tin bowls as she brought them down to the table.

He'd hear the sifting of the flour, the shaking of the salt, the stirring of the yeast in the honey-and-water.

And while the yeast was bubbling up to a froth, she'd stick her head round the door and ask "All right, dear?" and stick it back again without waiting for an answer, since he was usually buried too deep in his paper to reply.

She sighed to herself, and tied the apron tighter round her waist and higher round her neck to stop the flour from escaping to places it shouldn't on her blue print dress.

Once the froth had built up its good brown head, and was shivering high on top of the wrist-warm water, she tipped it into the well she'd dug inside the flour bowl, and scraped it wet and lumpy with her singed wooden spoon.

At first, nothing would happen. She'd hum to herself a chorale from the old German, round and round as round and round she stirred, always back to the beginning, and each beat of her spoon marking the beat of the hymn. Slowly, the mixture changed from lumpy sludge with pockets of dry flour still to be found and burst, to smooth and sticky. And the song changed with it, from breathless-bumpy to a slow, steady march.

But when the dough changed further, slow by slow, to a silkiness, yeastiness, stretch-and-milkiness, the song took on a new note – a high, piercing wail that cut through the kitchen and straight next door into the living room, so that her husband would finally have to get up and shut the door with a bang.

Now the dough was ready to be worked.

Her hands were large and capable. They wore the burns of oven-reaching, the scalds of hot pan-handling, the hacks of onion-chopping, and they wore them well and proudly. She could mend fences with those hands, change a tyre, split a log. They were hands for all seasons and every weather, and every hour of the day.

But not the night.

At night, her hands lay and rested against her sides, sleeping a grateful sleep along with the rest of her. And if they ever thought to wander in her dreams, across the bed to where other hands lay, and other arms joined to them, and attached to those a large, wheezing body, with a large, wheezing head at the top of it, they soon were wandered back again, and firmly replaced where they'd come from.

The dough had cleaned the bowl dry, picking up all the fallen bits of itself and taking them in, disappearing them into its own folds, where they were never seen again. She stopped singing the song, set the bowl aside and floured the table lightly. Then she slapped the dough straight down onto it in a single angry movement.

"Grrrr," she hissed, at the lump of dough, her face bent low towards it. There was no immediate reply. She could smell its heady smell, the not-quite-pleasant and not-quite-not smell that always pulled her close for a second opinion.

The dough sat there, deflated, flattened, a surprising dead weight for its size.

"Grrrr," she said again, and again it did what dough usually does.

Then she straightened up, and pulled up her sleeve, and raised her hand, angled to its sharpest side, and *slup!* whacked the dough with a karate chop that might have sliced it clean in half, if it hadn't been so chewy.

Instead, it lay there, dented.

Mmmmrrrrrmmmrrr went the slow growing growl in her throat. She grasped the dough by its twin hills and swivelled it 90° to the left. Again, she raised her hand, and before she knew it, the slow growing growl exploded in a mighty *yeaaahhh!*

The dough juddered, now double-dented, north-south and east-west, like an uncooked hot cross bun. This was the end of the first phase, and time for the chorale to kick in again, with a busy, no-nonsense tempo.

Turn *slup!* Turn *slup!* Turn *slup!* Turn *slup!*

The lump flattened gradually under the weight of its crosses into a ridged landscape reminiscent of a pizza.

When she could level it no more with the chopping, she grabbed it rudely in her fist, sank her nails deep into the cool, damp mass, and rolled it back into a ball.

Then began the kneading. She took the hard heel of her hand and ground it heavily into the dough, stretching it away from her till it thinned to transparency and burst into lacy holes. Once it had ripped raggedly in half, she scooped it all together again, stuffing the torn edges back into the mixture and folding it back into an approximate lump. Then s-t-r-e-t-ch and tear and s-t-r-e-t-c-h and tear, faster and faster, bouncing the chorale along as if it were the jauntiest folksong, until little by little, the dough began to feel supple as kid suede, and smoothed out beautifully to the colour and shape of a new puffball.

She stopped for a moment, tilted her head to the mushroom lump and listened. Nothing. The opening fanfare of the news jingled faintly through the wall. She wiped a wisp of hair from her eyes and turned back to the job in hand.

Next came the punching. She'd taken off her rings for kneading, since their scratchy gems and pointed claws tore off shreds of paste that took an age to pick out afterwards. But now she put them on again, the wedding and engagement rings on one hand, and on the other, three dress rings with clunky carbuncles that she kept solely for the purpose. She rolled her fists into tight knuckled balls, and began punching. She punched sharp, she punched hard. She punched tough, she punched mean. She punched fast, she punched dirty, upper cuts, under cuts, left hooks, right hooks, the rings each time dragging vicious scars across the dough until it was a sagging, beaten mess on the table.

Again she stopped, again she listened. All was quiet, except the muffled urgency of the television next door.

Next came the pounding. The knead-and-punching had twisted air into the dough, locking it into small hidden pockets that had to be found and stamped out. Slup *thud!*

Slup *thud!* Slup *thud!* She walloped it against the wooden worktop so hard you wondered it didn't crack it. With each thump came a small bursting breath, as the air was choked from its hiding place. *Sssss,* it sighed. *Ssssseee. Sssss.* It really was a most satisfying feeling.

It was only when the bubbles were almost gone, when the last pouch of life was being hunted down with deadly tenacity, that she finally heard what she was waiting for.

Merseee. Merseeee.

It came from inside, from the pulped yeast-flour-water. She bent down and turned her best ear towards it.

Mercy. Mercy.

Unmistakable. A faint whimper of air, almost too weak to catch. She smiled. At last. The dough was ready to prove.

She cradled it into a tidy ball and set it back in the metal bowl, covering the top with a damp tea towel.

Next door, the news was just finishing. There was an hour to go before tea-time, the oven already roasting the beef joint within, and only small busy things to be doing. She stuck her head round the door.

"All right?"

Her husband was bending over, just about to pick up the paper and rebury his head in the business section. Seizing her moment, she rounded the sofa and stood oh-so-casually right on top of the supplement. He looked up, finding himself face-to-face with the floury smears of her apron. The familiar yeasty smell clung to her hands and all the rest of her.

She dropped a kiss onto his smooth, bony head.

"Glad to hear it!" she sang. "I'm all right, too. Never been better!"

And she creaked down on her knees and rested her arms across his lap to look straight into his eyes.

His eyes were elsewhere. His eyes were on the move, unreachable, uncatchable, unreadable, however much she stared.

For he raised his head and he ducked his head, strained to the left, strained to the right, tilted and squinted this way and that, trying all the time to look past her at the television, where someone was explaining in a chirpy voice what would fill that space for the rest of the night.

It was enough. She grabbed his face between her two hands and gripped it tight and still.

"Tonight, maybe?" Her voice was full of longing. She leaned forward and brushed her lips to his.

And still his eyes – trapped in their sockets, trapped in turn between the two capable hands – wandered up and down, right and left, through her and past her to where a chirpy voice squeaked about time and the filling of it.

"You're blocking the view," he said, through squashed jaws. She felt them grind stiffly beneath her palms.

{70}

"Sorry," she said, and stood up. There was a mark of flour on his lap where she'd leaned her powdery apron against him. She leaned forward to brush it off. Her hand met his, also brushing – brushing her large self from his view of the small bright box behind her.

As she closed the kitchen door behind her, he looked up, just for an instant.

"Tomorrow," he whispered. She was a good woman. He was lucky to have her.

In the kitchen, the dough had crawled up the sides of the bowl, stretching itself thin and thinner in the heat, reaching the suffocating towel and pushing out beyond and over the lip. It was a foam, a mousse, a lightness, lifted by bubbles to meet the air above.

She saw that it had risen. Good. She stripped the cloth from the bowl. The dough collapsed back inside, deflated. She gathered the soft scraps into a floppy ball and slapped it back on the table.

Walnuts. Crisp, scratchy walnuts. She shook the packet onto the table and rolled the dough around in it, grinding them good and sure into every corner.

Caraway. Tart, biting caraway. She shivered a couple of tablespoons into the mix and pummelled it through furiously.

She oiled a baking tray and opened the oven door. The heat stung her face, and carried the sizzle and smell of roast into the kitchen. Quickly, she slammed it shut and turned the temperature up.

Then she shaped the dough into a flattened round and laid it on the baking tray, cutting a north-south, east-west cross in the surface.

The oven thermometer clicked. The red light went off. It was ready. She opened the door and lowered the tray slowly, carefully towards the top, hottest shelf.

The roast spat and sputtered its boiling juices onto the oven floor, where they fizzed and turned to black.

Sssss. Seeee. Merseeee, hissed the small round loaf, as the oven door closed on it with a click. And through the glass door, it could be seen minute by minute stretching itself up, gradually rising on each side of its cut cross, into four peaks that slowly browned to stiffness.

She watched. She watched and picked the paste from her fingers.

Later, when they broke the loaf in four and dipped it in the gravy from the sizzling roast, he wondered why, with all the kneading and pounding and mashing and mauling, and above all, with all the practice every night of every week of every year since time he could remember, her baking always weighed as heavy in his gut as a lump of sodden stone.

Ally McMahon's New Wife

WHEN ALLY McMAHON woke up that morning, he knew something was wrong with his wife. He could hear her downstairs in the kitchen, making the breakfast. He could smell – could it be? – fresh coffee, and hear the special dinner-party coffee machine sishing to itself like a pint-size geyser. And beyond, singed at the edges, was another smell that wrapped itself around the coffee and climbed the stairs and through the door, into the bedroom where he lay.

Toast? No, not quite. He sniffed harder, taking in a chestful of the warm half-burnt aroma. Something baked? She never baked. Something fried? Yes – he heard the sudden sizzle of whatever was landing in the frying pan, curling at the edges, shrivelling itself into – pancakes?

He sucked in another lungful. Yes, pancakes, or something very like it. The pancake-waft coiled itself around the coffee-waft and danced under his nose. Unmistakeable. You didn't forget that smell, even if you hadn't come across it these twenty years.

They were cereal people. Always. A bowlful of sawdust and a dribble of semi-skimmed in the morning. A quick cup of instant, a shower and shave, twin squirts to the armpits, then teeth, hair, nose and shoes and out the house with a minute to spare. That was how it was.

Something was the matter with Janet. He leaned across the bed and looked at the clock. 7.15. She was never up before 8. By the sounds of it, she'd been up for a good hour. You couldn't rush pancakes. That much he remembered.

"Janet!" he shouted. "Is that you?"

"Helloooo!" sang a voice of such sun and sweetness he couldn't immediately place it. Janet? It didn't sound like her at all. She was always a girny cow before 11. They always breakfasted in silence, slouched behind their separate cereal boxes.

He put on his dressing gown and padded downstairs. The kitchen table was set for two, with a jug of orange juice in the middle, and a jug – a jug! – of milk beside it. There were napkins by each plate, and teacups with proper saucers, instead of mugs.

Janet was at the hob, wearing a good dress and a green checked pinny.

"Just in time!" She turned and flew her arms around him, holding the sticky wooden spatula aloft. Her fresh-washed hair fell against his cheek like a perfumed scarf. Her legs pressed firmly against him. It felt odd, like touching a limb deadened by sleep.

Then she turned and flipped a pancake onto a plate, and sprinkled it with brown – brown! – sugar and a squeeze of real lemon from a crystal press he'd never seen. She folded it into quarters and sat it down at his place and licked her fingers.

He watched, nervously.

"What are you waiting for?" She turned back to the hob and swung another ladleful of batter into the pan.

It wasn't his wife. He was suddenly sure. Whoever it was, it wasn't Janet. She looked the same, she sounded the same, she moved, smelled and felt the same, but otherwise she couldn't have been more different.

He craned to see the red spot on her neck – the one that itched for rain and throbbed for snow. Yes, it was there, all right. But still, it didn't fool him. It wasn't her. It was as though a different soul had been decanted inside her body. One that sang and stirred batter as though it had never known otherwise. One that made her hips sway like a fine fat calf's.

He sat down and ate. The pancakes tasted crisp and buttery. If his wife had been replaced, he wasn't too sure he wanted to complain.

When he had finished, he stood up to do the dishes.

"Don't worry. I'll do those." She tweaked the dishcloth from his hand and flicked it playfully at his rear.

"Come on, now," he protested. "That's enough."

"Enough what?" Her smile speared right into him. He stared at those blank, unknown eyes, and found that he couldn't move.

"Who are you?" he whispered.

"Does it matter?" she asked, coquettishly. Behind the smile, her eyes gleamed like a snake's.

He tried to swallow. His mouth was drier than a sandstorm.

"You're taking liberties," he croaked. "This is my house."

"I like it here," she said. "Nice front garden, decent kitchen, handy for the shops. There's plenty of room for both of us. And out there" – she gestured to the window – "a view to die for."

She stood at the window and gazed across the fields. They were gold as lions in the still-deep sun, the hills paling in folds behind. A bank of larches lined the horizon like a crewcut. Birds wove overhead, dipping and ducking against the sky. McMahon peered over her shoulder. They'd bought the house for the view, it was true. They'd never got round to putting up curtains.

She leaned on the windowsill and stared out, her chin resting on her floury fist, the spatula clutched in her hand.

"I could stay here forever."

"You can't do that," he said, quickly. "The neighbours will talk."

"They won't," she smiled. "They'll never know."

And she turned her attention to the frying pan, now spitting fat onto the hotplate.

McMahon was troubled all day at work. He hoped that when he returned, he'd find his real wife sitting there, the grim old grouchbag, and he'd be able to peck her cheek and see her rub away the kiss as usual.

Then he'd ask, "what's for tea?" and she'd say "the usual" and they'd sit down to fish fingers and beans and get on with how it was.

But Janet wasn't there. In her place was the new one, smiling her odd stretched smile, and putting the finishing touches to a pink mousse swimming in yellow sauce.

"Still here?" he said.

"Oh yes. I'm going nowhere, dear." Janet never said 'dear'. The closest she ever got was 'our dad', though they didn't have children, for reasons that had never been discussed.

The new wife stuck a mint leaf into the mousse and stepped back to admire it. "I've had a gorgeous day, thank you. How about you?"

McMahon sat down and picked up a spoon. The mousse cut like a cloud. He stirred it around in the lemony sauce.

"Where's Janet?"

Before she could reply, he'd spluttered the mousse into his spoon. Fish. Smoked salmon. He'd expected sweetness. He pushed the plate away and stood up, finding himself closer to her face than he'd intended.

"I don't know what you're playing at, but I want my wife back."

She bent and kissed his cheek, smelling of fish and lemon.

"Ally, you're tired. Why don't you come to bed?"

She'd said his name. Janet never said his name, except when she was spoiling for a fight. Then he'd hear it as soon as he walked in the front door. "Alasdair?" she'd say, with a little curling question mark at the end. And he'd take a deep breath and go through to the living room and trouble.

"Ally." Her fingers were stroking his sideburns, his ear, his neck, his lips. "Ally McMahon."

He found himself taken by the hand and led to the foot of the stairs, and up the first stair, and the second, and somehow all the way up onto the landing and through the door and onto the bed, where he lay flat on his back, swallowing as she undid him, stroked him and twisted Janet's body in new and undignified ways. He watched her fling her legs and arch her back and toss her hair around her face like someone from a late-night film. He couldn't stop her. Whenever she fixed him with those dark, blank eyes, all the will drained right out him.

And later, amid all the fists and fight and fury, he gasped out Janet! Janet! Janet! three times, each time quieter than the last, she nodded and closed those eyes, sinking back on her haunches with a shudder.

It was only afterwards, when she lay there asleep, her arms flopped across the bed, her breathing slow and even, that he remembered that his wife had gone.

The next day early, McMahon went to the police.

"I'd like to report a missing person," he said. "My wife. Last seen the day before yesterday."

The duty officer took some notes. "You're confident she's actually missing?"

"Definite. We haven't spent a night apart for twenty years." He leaned across the desk and whispered close to the officer's hairy ear. "The trouble is –"

"Yes?"

"Someone else has moved in. Someone who looks very like her. So like her, only a close friend could tell the difference."

"A twin?"

"In a manner of speaking. An imposter."

"Mr McMahon, I should warn you that if you're found to be wasting police time –"

McMahon's hand flew out and grabbed the policeman's lapel.

"I've never been in trouble. You can look me up on your list. I won't be there. Not even a parking fine. I don't know why she's doing this. I've never done anything to anyone. I just want it back to how it was."

"All right, Mr McMahon. Don't distress yourself. We'll send someone round for a chat."

McMahon straightened up and stared at the wall. "I found her making pancakes," he said. "That's when I first suspected. I don't expect you to understand that. That you could know someone so well, so inside out and upside down, that you know they would never make pancakes. Not now, not for the rest of all their lives. It's a small thing, but significant. Don't you see? Pancakes is something other people do, but never Janet. It wasn't in her nature. It couldn't be, ever. That's how well I knew her. And so to find her doing so was a moment of horror. Because then I knew it wasn't her at all. It was someone else, wearing her body."

"Mr McMahon, have you been at the drink?"

"Teetotal. That's me. You can test me if you like. You can cut bits of my hair. You won't find a trace of it. The pinkest liver in the country."

Beneath the desk, the officer rang a bell.

"I think it's time we took you back home."

"Yes, do that. Then I can show you. We can devise some tests. She won't be able to keep it up for ever."

He smiled at the officer with what he hoped was his sanest, most intelligent smile.

When they reached his home, the new wife was sitting in the kitchen, peeling apples. She looked up, anxiously. The policeman took off his cap and nodded in a friendly manner.

Wrapped Town

"Mrs McMahon?"

"Ally! I've been that worried! Oh, officer, I'm relieved you've found him."

She rushed over and gave him the familiar too-tight hug.

"Here we go," said McMahon. "The patter."

"Is your husband well, Mrs McMahon?"

"Has he been havering again?" She ruffled McMahon's head as though he were a six-year-old.

"Hang on a minute!" said McMahon. "None of that talking about me as though I'm no here! It was me went to the police, and I'm counting on backup."

The new wife sighed and pointed to a chair.

"You'd better sit down, officer. What's he been saying now?"

"Mainly that you're not his wife."

"Oh, Ally," she tutted. She gestured to the photo on the sideboard. There he stood with Janet: she in a white wedding gown, he in a kilt and jacket.

"And what does that prove, eh?" said McMahon. "That you look like Janet, nothing more. And you do, I'll give you that. To the very plook on your neck and the very scar on your hip-bone."

"I'm sure the officer wants to know that, dear."

"Just keep an open mind. That's all I'm asking." McMahon grasped the policeman's hand fiercely. "Because she's a devil, this one. Threats and intimidation the minute your back's turned. She's here for the duration, she says, whether I like it or not. She's taken over the kitchen and she's done away with Janet."

The policeman made a few notes in his notebook.

"That's a serious allegation, Mr McMahon."

"It's a serious crime. Janet has been abducted, presumably without her will. This woman has studied her every move and manner and walked straight into her life without the slightest qualm. She must have been studying her for years. Stalking us. Practising her speech and actions in front of a mirror. It doesn't bear thinking about. And where's Janet all this time? Why haven't I heard from her? Her disappearance is completely out of character and I have to assume the worst."

The officer scribbled some more and turned to the new wife.

"Mrs McMahon?"

"No!" shouted McMahon, crashing his fist on the kitchen table. The cups rattled in their saucers. "I won't have it. See – you're already on her side. Taking her word for it. Giving her the benefit. She isn't Mrs McMahon, and there's no one better to judge that than me."

The policeman ignored the outburst. "Ma'am. Perhaps you'd be kind enough to give me the name of your family doctor?"

"As if she'd know!" spat McMahon. "She's only waltzed into the house these past couple of days."

Her smile was sweet and tired.

"Dr Armstrong. We've been with him for years."

The officer nodded and wrote it down. "I'll be going, then. Someone will be in touch. If you've any trouble in the meantime, give us a call." He addressed his remark carefully to the middle of the room. Then he shut his notebook and went.

McMahon sat down and was still for a moment. He didn't look at her.

"So what now?"

"I think it's time you saw the doctor, dear."

"Don't dear me. Janet never deared me, and you're not starting now. What have you done with her? Where is she?"

The new wife was standing behind him at the sink. He didn't notice the scissors until it was too late. In one quick movement, she whipped up the flap of his jacket and snipped. A length of wire tumbled down and dangled to his knees.

"Amateur," she hissed. "Think you'd get me with a daft trick like that? I'm ahead of you, Ally McMahon. Always will be. I can see right into your bony little head, and don't forget it. And you can put that knife down. It won't do any good."

McMahon flinched, nicking his thumb on the thin vegetable knife he'd been cradling in his pocket.

"I can give you things, mm?" she said, close to his ear. "Nice things. Things to eat, things to see, things to enjoy. Just relax and we'll work it out."

{83}

He swallowed. "Janet," he said. He'd meant it as a question, but it came out as a fact. She nodded.

"That's right, Ally dear. Janet. We'll get along much better if you just take it in your stride."

And she took the knife from his pocket and put it in the drawer.

That night, she led him upstairs and kept her word. As he watched her bounce above him, he did at times wonder whether he'd lost something – not Janet, not control, but a sense of who and where he was. Maybe he'd been told about all this in advance, and simply forgotten? Maybe notification had come in the post and was now buried somewhere below a pile of bills or junkmail? Maybe there was a crucial TV programme he'd missed, or a paper he'd failed to buy, or maybe he just didn't socialise enough to keep abreast of things? He felt out of step with the world, as though he'd walked off a cliff and found not the terrifying freefall he'd been warned about, but an invisible current that kept him aloft and walking, always dazed and always worried, yet unable to stop or look down.

He lay awake. She was asleep, stretched out naked in that free way that even then told him she wasn't his wife. Janet was all crunched knees in bed, all elbows and tightly pulled covers, as though the merest chink of air below the duvet would give her pneumonia. And she wore clothes – fleece two-pieces in winter and, in summer, long nighties in shiny stuff that hanked on his skin.

The new wife lay open. Her arms and legs were splayed across the bed. Her hair fell across her pillow and halfway onto his. Her mouth gaped. It was the first chance he'd had to take a good long look. She had fine teeth. He'd forgotten that. Far back, he could see the one silver filling she'd had done two years ago. Her tongue lay still in its curved setting of teeth. He thought of the knife and of touching it to her throat, pressing little by little until the point slit her skin.

Now would be the time, and here the place.

He could use his hands. Her neck was thin. With his two hands around it and his weight on top, he'd easily keep his grip. It was only a matter of – two minutes? Three? Four? As long as he locked his hands and kept his nerve, and looked perhaps the other way while her face changed.

He raised himself up on his elbow and watched her closely, seeing how her nostrils stretched and slackened with every breath. She seemed to be whistling. Yes, he could hear a high whistle pass through her, only ever outways, from deep in her throat. It seemed to be rhythmic, as though it were lodged on a bit of phlegm or mucus.

It was then that he heard the voice. His wife's. Janet's. Small and weak, but clearly recognisable.

"Alasdair!" she was calling. "Alasdair!" He looked around in the half-dark, eased himself silently to the edge of the bed so that he could look beneath it. No, she was quieter there. She was somewhere close by, though calling so feebly he'd almost missed it.

He leaned across the new wife to search the other side of the bed. As he bent towards her, the voice grew louder.

"Alasdair! In here!"

He bent his ear close to the sleeping mouth. "Alasdair!" There it was again. Her tiny, needling voice. It was coming from far down inside the new wife's throat.

"Janet," he whispered. "Is that you?"

"Who else would it be?" snapped the thin wee voice.

"Are you okay?"

"What do you think?" she said, in some exasperation. "Are you going to do something about it, or are you going to sit there on your fat end as usual?"

"I don't know what to do. No one will believe me," he said.

"Huh. You get them down here and I'll soon tell them what to believe." The voice rose to a new pitch of indignation. "She's not getting away with this, I'm telling you. You should see it in here. The state of it. Not fit for a dog. She might be all ticky-dory on the outside, but she's a downright scunner in here."

The new wife stirred in sleep, mumbling incoherently to herself. For a while, the voice was trapped behind her lips.

McMahon wiped his brow on a corner of duvet. What could he do? He thought of his recording machine, lying useless in the kitchen bin. He wondered whether he could open the lips without waking the rest of the body. But the new wife's mouth gaped open, and again he could hear Janet, squeaking on where she'd left off.

"Do something, Alasdair," she said. "I can't stay here much longer. It's not right."

He felt a sudden lump in his throat at her bravery. "I love you, Janet," he whispered. As soon as he'd spoken, he put his hand to his mouth. He'd never said those words like that. Not with her name at the end and all. It felt strange and hopeless.

The voice climbed to an almost inaudible pitch.

"You and your fancy talk! I'll give you love, I will. You that's been humping and hawing all over her, and me only gone these two days."

There was a pause. When she spoke again, she sounded so far away he had to strain to catch her at all.

"I'm divorcing you, Alasdair. As soon as I get out of here. I'm sorry, but that's how it has to be. I've got every grounds and I won't hear any arguments."

He waited, but it seemed she'd finished what she had to say.

"I'm sorry," he said. "I didn't know."

"Don't give me that. You knew all right. I'm disappointed in you, Alasdair McMahon. Very disappointed."

He felt tears tickling his eyes. He knew she was right. She usually was.

But her voice had thinned to a whistle of air, and his ears were full of heartbeat, drumming her out.

It was beyond him, like everything else. He'd keep walking the current, walking while it held, with the terrifying cliff and the sea-crashing rocks below.

McMahon's new wife twitched in her sleep. Her lips clicked, tasting a memory.

He stroked her chin and watched as she closed her mouth and turned to face the wall.

Loose Muse Walking

GATHER ROUND CLOSE, and make room at the back. Keep quiet and don't touch anything. And whatever you do, don't make any sudden movements. They're easily startled.

So. Here we are. Very lucky indeed. Native habitat, almost pristine. If we keep still for long enough, we might catch a sighting. A highly endangered species, the working poet.

Caution at the front there: words at work. Beware of flying adjectives, stray nouns, verbs on the loose, and adverbs. Especially adverbs.

You're right. It doesn't look like a poetic sort of place. Not even in the quaint, dilapidated way that Sunday supplements coo over – the picturesque poverty of cracked paint and peeling floral wallpaper.

No, it just looks averagely grim, in a way that will never be fashionable, even for boxrooms. Look at those squares of paleness on the walls. Pictures. Or, at least, the places where pictures used to be, protecting the paint from its slow decline from magnolia to smoky ochre. See the old mosaiced lino on the floor, with a round toilet pedestal cutout in memory of the bathroom it came from. No curtains. Just a sheet, drawing-pinned across the window. A chair, a table, a rubber plant straggling from its pot.

Nothing to inspire the soul. Nothing to lift the spirit, even an inch or two.

Nonetheless, this is where one of the nation's best-paid poets plies his trade.

Shoosh and still! For here he comes, right on cue, creaking open the door with a heavy sigh.

Charity Wise.

It's not his real name, of course. He chose it, with a bit of help from his wife, Maureen. Charity for generosity, a waft of old-fashioned religion and a subliminal pitch for the sympathy vote. Wise for Morecambe, where he was born, but also for essence of earth mother, ample lap and bosom, the comfort hug, the homespun serenity that comes from age and the realisation that all that youthful leaping around was pretty much a waste of time.

Charity Wise. Diddly-da. The very rhythm combines artless optimism with solid reassurance. A frivolous skip, then a firm stride – something to lighten the heart and give it strength. A name to remember.

Better than Bert, anyroad. So British. So prose.

Wrapped Town

The Charity Wise Friendship Calendar has been around for twenty years. Each one a masterpiece, and each one a bestseller. He hangs in more of the nation's homes than *If*. He's sat on more mantelpieces, appeared on more tea towels, and yes, shifted more books than any other poet of his generation.

Take a look, then, at this solid optimist, this frivolous rock with the Midas touch.

Judging by the teeth, he's fifty-five or so, with hair in the process of vacating his brow and retreating to somewhere further back, out of the wind. A comfortable face dyed pink by a lifetime of beer. A nose to match. Wild, springy brows that surely impede an easy view of the sky, especially when they're furrowed, as now.

He places his kit on the table, item by item, like a careful waiter: A pad of Basildon Bond (ruled, feint) and a Bic biro (fine, blue). A rhyming dictionary and a can of Tennants (open, half-empty). From his shirt pocket he extracts a packet of Embassy Tipped (two left) and a Bic lighter (disposable). See how he balances them upright, on their ends. They fall over several times, but he perseveres. Finally, they're whipped into line and ready. All he needs now is inspiration.

His breathing is heavy. He stares downward at the pad of paper, scarcely blinking. He shuts his eyes and screws up his nose. There's a visible heaving and a straining going on in there, beneath his skull. Will he find it, whatever it is? Will he connect the connections that open the floodgate and pour the poetry onto his page? Who knows? He certainly doesn't look happy. He even looks a bit tortured.

Those of you who find this disturbing may leave. The rest may sit down and eat their packed lunches.

Minutes pass. Nothing. Not a flicker in the lightbulb department. Nothing stirs, save a spider abseiling from the lampshade. The shaft of light from the window inches closer to the next lozenge on the lino. The only sound is the in-rasp and out-rasp of Charity's breathing, as oxygen and carbon dioxide cycle endlessly between him and the gangly rubber plant.

Inspiration. Expiration. In. Out.

While we're waiting, let's recap.

A fortnight ago, Bert's wife, Maureen, was on her knees, rootling under the bed for her good heels to go to Cousin Edith's girl's wedding. She'd hauled out the trunk of spare sheets, and was down and deep and dusty in the far back corner when her fingers found a plastic bag. A new one, light and squashy, like a cushion. One not listed in her comprehensive mental inventory. Curious, she dragged it out to get a better look.

It wasn't her usual sort of bag – the cheap and crinkly white sort with words that slanted to the right, as if they were in some tremendous hurry. No, it was a black bag from a bookshop, smooth and smart, bearing gold letters with impeccable upright posture.

A present? Unlikely. Not Bert. Fat chance he'd suddenly learn the art of surprise after twenty-five years of marriage.

She sat up and shook the contents onto the carpet, where they fell in a floppy, tangled heap. As she lifted them up for closer inspection, the corners of her mouth drooped southward, and slow, plump tears brimmed from her eyes and blinked down her nose onto her blouse, drenching the cotton daisies.

A heavy ash blond wig, thick and moptop. An outsize bra the colour of an anaemic peach. Two pairs of walking socks rolled into balls. Stretchy white knickers as big as a pillow case. A pair of huge suspenders still hooked up to thick, tan stockings that bulged extravagantly at the knees and heels, in memory of the legs they'd recently encased.

A lipstick. A loud, pillarbox lipstick. Real Chanel. Maureen opened it and sniffed. It smelled rich and glossy, of silk and chiffon. The tip was worn to a kiss-shaped point.

And an overall. Her overall – the stripy crisp work one she'd been missing all these years.

She sat there on the carpet for more than an hour, listening to the wind thrum the telegraph wires. Then, though it was only two in the afternoon, she got up, undressed, put on her brushed cotton chin-high nighty and went to bed, which is where Bert found her.

A cold, she said at first, sniffling under the covers, the piles of scruffy Kleenex littering the bed. A week later, it's a bad dose of the flu, and dead and dying tissues have colonized her cardigan sleeve all the way up to the raglan seam.

And now, a fortnight on, it's looking like pneumonia, with drifts of sopping hanky nesting under the pillow, and breeding and disintegrating in every corner of the room.

Deep in her duvet cocoon, Maureen is drinking Lemsip by the vat, sucking the strong fumes through the mush of her head. It isn't doing much good, save to send her to sleep in the daytime. The doctor has been and found nothing wrong, though he agrees she's not her usual self, what with the red eyes and the tendency to burst out crying every few minutes. Take it easy, he says, and gives her a bottle of pills to be going on with.

She guards the bed and its bag like a watchdog. She only gets up for trips to the bathroom, as few and fast as she can make them.

At night, she lies stiffly awake on her back, flinching whenever her husband's extremities brush against her in his sleep. The nuzzle of his chin against her firmly ribboned neck sets off pictures too dreadful to contemplate.

Her dreams are filled with giants – thickset shapes in overalls, stotting on cobbles with moptop hair. Giants that turn and have air for faces.

Under their bed, in the fat black bag, lie the various parts of Charity Wise, trapped by a thick layer of mattress and an unknown illness that doesn't look like shifting.

Maureen lies above, damp and exhausted, unwilling to confront her, and unable to let her out.

Meanwhile, downstairs, there's been a breakthrough of sorts. Suddenly, without warning, the poet takes his pen and writes a line.

To a Special Someone

This he embellishes with underlining, bolding, boxing-in, flowers and curlicues, executed with far more care and attention than a weary cliché strictly deserves.

Even the poet knows it's not an original line. He didn't invent it. He didn't even reinvent it and claim it as his own, as some of his colleagues are prone to do.

Yes, well spotted – it's an E15. A *Special Someone*. A sentiment with a stock code all its own. In the display rack it lives six from the right, next to *New Home* and *Sorry You're Leaving* (*humour*).

Bert is sweating, and no wonder. Special Someones are hard to pin down. What do they look like? How old are they? Where do they live? What do they eat? What do they wear? Do they like Perry Como? Do they walk or drive? The answers are as many as the people on the streets. We're all Special Someones to someone.

For Charity, there's a big deadline up ahead. It's January – the high season of the stationery world. Time to plan the Christmas calendars. Not for this year, mind, but for the next and those thereafter.

Think of that, while you're slumped on your sofa like a slug, digesting turkey, channel-flicking from one bonhomie to the indistinguishable next. The Christmas you'll buy next year is already out there, tensed and waiting on the starting blocks. And before the Queen can even draw breath – Ding! Ching! Cards, candles, tinsel, lights! They're off, overtaking on the inside, bounding into the world of commerce in their gaudy satins and glitters and golds. Reps have pitched their bets, retailers placed their orders, wholesalers cleared their shelf space. They know what you want. They know what you will buy a year from now. And you will. Count on it.

January, then, finds Bert under pressure. His round face accordingly shines a redder shade of pink, and his brows are drawn so low you wonder he can even see the window, much less the sky beyond.

A brain scan would reveal increased activity in the temporal lobes, a frenzied flashing of synapses as he attempts to force the delicate rhubarb of inspiration. The only outward manifestation is a new doodle – a childish flower, petals round like thumbs. He gives it two eyes and an automatic smiling mouth, then frowns, shuts the smile across the top and adds a couple of fangs. Four sides of a prison box around it all, and a scribble of bars. More bars, sharp and steely. You can just make out the face behind them, all fangs and petals. It's not his strong point, drawing. More bars, thicker and angrier, until there's nothing to see but pen.

It's not happening for him. Something's gone, it seems. No surprises, no ideas. His mind's as dull as cardboard, though he can usually write poems standing on his head. Twelve inspirations is all it takes, one a month to hang on the wall.

Special Someone. Special Someone, he mutters, viciously. See how he shuts his eyes tight, squeezing his brain to wring the dregs of life from it.

When he opens them, he finds he's written a word on the pad: *fright. Frightfright*, he writes. *Frightfrightfright*. It has a pleasing shape, swelling and looping in just the right places. *Frightfrightfrightfright*.

Where did it come from, this word? The same place as all the others. Somewhere deep and hidden. Somewhere, unfortunately, that can't be found by looking.

Maureen. Maureen, Maureen, tossing in her bed above the fragrant bag of bits. Such pictures in her head! Such imaginings! Things she'd only heard about from other people's lives. Things that could never belong to hers.

Lipstick smooth against a rough, chapped mouth. Stockings snagged on a hairy thigh. Ash curls bouncing on a sandpaper cheek. A cheek she'd stroked, a thigh she'd squeezed, a mouth she'd kissed.

And her overall, the crisp stripy work one, stretched to bursting across a chest broad as a wardrobe. Bert's chest, with all its fur and flatness, and no shape at all to sit in the deep stitched darts.

She thinks of the long hours, the locked door, the meals left outside and eaten too cold to enjoy. The "do not disturb" sign and the inspiration – the slippery ghost that came and went as it wanted, seemingly, and couldn't be summoned. It was a strange job, right enough. Stranger than ever she'd suspected.

Who is he? And who was he, all the years since her overall upped and offed? She doesn't know what to think. She doesn't know what to feel.

He called her his muse. She liked that, though she didn't believe him. He usually said it when he was feeling frisky, and since frisky was the nearest he ever got to romantic, it had to do.

Naturally, she's toned down her expectations over the years, mapping her ideal man as well as she can onto the one she married. She doesn't want perfection. She's even given up on great, and as good as it gets, and not bad considering. She's been happy enough with solid. But to find the solid crumbling before her eyes into a bag of cobbled parts – that's unbearable.

Wrapped Town

As she half-sits, half-lies in her hanky-strewn bed, the Lemsip blasts a path through her scrambled brain. She considers her options.

Quickly discarding death – his, hers, both – as too messy and impossible, and too prone to attention from unwanted quarters, she wonders about simply staying put.

It would have to be forever, if at all. It would involve bedsores and wasted muscles. Even breakfast in bed would surely lose its charm after a while. The doctor would lose patience if he kept on finding nothing wrong.

But at least the bag would stay put, the infernal bag of parts. And maybe the mice would get it – burrow inside and bite it into nothings to line their nests.

Or there was fire. A quick match struck and flung. The plastic would burn fast, and shrivel onto the polyester curls and melt them. Yes, fire would be an option.

Back downstairs, Bert's frowning in concentration, still as a poacher ready to pounce.

An idea is lurking on the outskirts of his head. He feels it flash past with a glimmer of promise – a shadow, a shiver, a taste of something. It's sitting there, just out of reach, like a dream just dreamt, but still close enough to catch if he strains his all.

He shuts his eyes tight and inches towards it, slowly, hoping desperately that the phone won't ring or the next door's dog bark. It's still there, gleaming faintly, a shapeless wisp swaying on the edge of focus.

Careful now. Gently does it. Think hard. Harder.

Suddenly, the idea flares into view and crystallizes to a shape, clear and naked as a flame.

Bert takes a flying leap and hooks and reels it into his conscious. It's a beauty, wriggling with life. He struggles to hold it still.

Then he crumples his hopeless scribbles into a ball and lobs them into the corner. A fresh new page for a fresh new thought, gifted from beyond knows where.

In a large, confident hand, he writes the words again:

To a Special Someone

Then he leans back and stretches out his shoulders, savouring the excitement of the moment. It's a good feeling. A start. A breakthrough. A winner, even.

He bends to the paper and writes:

Our friendship is a garden
Full of special flowers

Not bad. Not bad at all. It has the germ of something.

Though come to think of it, doesn't it ring a bell? That rhythm. That pace. That trademark use of metaphor. Then he remembers: the Charity Wise Friendship Calendar, July '84:

Our friendship is a sunbeam
Full of special light

And what about October '97, the special car edition?

Our friendship is a motor car
Full of... full of...

What was it now?

Full of furry shite, he thinks. Dogs and dice dangling from the wing mirror. So big you can hardly see out. Killers, those things. And if they don't get you, sure as day you'll poison your lungs with a whiff of cardboard pinetree –

Woah! Discipline! Concentration! He hates the way his mind drops a beauty then wanders off, looking for mud to wallow in.

Our friendship is a garden
Full of special flowers
de-DA de-DA de-DA de-DA
de-DA de-DA de –

It used to be so easy.

... bowers, cowers, glowers...

He didn't have to fight.

... hours, powers, scours...

He didn't even have to try.

... showers, towers...

Towers?

de-DA-de-Fawlty Towers.

Not when he was dressed for the part.

de-DA-de-Eiffel –
JEEZ-oh!

Charity Wise. Up there under the bed. His muse. Suffocating slowly.

April showers. Shower powers. Power showers. Great things, right enough, power showers. Imagine having more than a trickle on your back in winter. Need to fix the back boiler first, though. Piece of nonsense, filling kettles for the dishes when you've a perfectly good coal fire –

It's no use. He goes next door to the bathroom to clean his ears with a cottonbud. While he's there, he notices that the grout needs scrubbing. Over the months, it's sprouted a rash of black dots, starting in the corner and marching all the way across to the soap dish. He picks a splayed toothbrush from the jar and starts scouring.

Half an hour later, he's still there, stood in the bath with his shoes on, squeezing the last of the toothpaste onto the tiles. As he smears it down the grout, he suddenly stops to ask the question that has troubled his subconscious for the past fortnight.

Does she know? Does Maureen know?

*

Upstairs, she has written off fire. It would melt not only the bag and all its nylon contents, but also the very house they live in, and Maureen herself, who'd be too slow to escape down the stairs after a fortnight's worth of weakened, unused legs.

Flight has also been ruled out. She and Bert don't have a joint account, and Maureen doesn't have private means to fund such an unnecessary, lonely drama. Plus there's always the tiniest possibility that the appearance of a bagful of Bert-fragranced women's clothing has a perfectly rational explanation. By fleeing, Maureen would never know.

There remains only confrontation. That could take several forms, viz.:

The overt, confrontational confrontation. Haul the bag of parts from its hideyhole, spread it on the bed like a bridal shower, point and say, "well?"

This would lead to confessions, tears and recriminations, stamping of feet, beating of fists and – hopefully – explanation and catharsis. Then Bert would promise not to do it again, and remove the bag to a place far away from sight and memory.

Or the sneaky, non-confrontational confrontation. Wear the overall. Extract it from its package, wash it at 90°C to remove all traces of masculine impregnation and put it on. Wear it about the house, casually to breakfast, business-like to lunch, and see what happens.

Either he says something, and dares to open up the whole sordid can of invertebrates, or he says nowt, all the while knowing that she knows he knows she knows, but keeping the whole fraught question under wraps.

Or the middle way: the void. The non-confrontational non-confrontation. Remove the bag and its disturbing contents and fling far away, bagged inside another black bag which, in turn, is bagged inside another. Fill the space with pillows, or cushions, or an empty suitcase, or a former toaster box full of rattling polystyrene. Then wait. Wait for nothing. Wait forever. He won't raise it, if he's any sense. The whole fraught question will be unwrapped, yes, but will hover invisibly between them, where anyone with grace and tact would do well to ignore it.

Maureen chases the options around the whirling flowchart in her head and falls into restless sleep.

Deep in her dream (let's look), giants lumber through cobbled streets, their kitten heels clackclacking. Their muscled calves bulge like bottles, the thick hair matted beneath tan 30 denier nylons.

All over the town, black plastic bags are on the move, wrinkling along the cobbles, unseen by the giant heels that stalk above them and pierce them now and then with a sigh. The bags stop in gathering swarms at the traffic lights, rustling quietly, cross the road at the signal change, and head for the town centre.

They merge from east and west into a seething convoy of plastic bags, strewn with gold letters that whirr above them and come to rest like butterflies, forming words – *wit, must, clip, fond, succulent, gorgeous.*

Their contents spill onto the street and join the march: rubber noses bouncing, false nails tripping, scarlet lips sucking along like slugs, long blonde tresses crimping, bushy wigs scuttling along the pavement, chased by hectic empty stockings that struggle against the wind.

Maureen watches the procession pass, hugging her shopping bag to her as it strains to join the others. Gradually, the rustle of plastic fades to the distance, as the convoy turns the corner out of sight. Relieved, she turns for home.

Behind her, waiting with outstretched arms, is a crisp, stripy overall that bends and wraps its sleeves around her, enveloping her in a snug embrace.

It feels warm. The kind of warmth that spreads all up and down her body, waking places that haven't stirred in years.

Maureen shrieks and sits bolt upright in the damp, sweaty bed.

✱

Get Well Soon

writes Bert, on the Basildon pad. He has to get Maureen out of there. The tragedy queen. The wet weekend. The doctor says there's nothing wrong with her. Time she got a grip.

> *I'm sad to hear you're poorly.*
> *I'm sad to hear you're ill.*
> *I hope it isn't catching.*
> *I hope you've writ your will.*

A deadline so tight he's choking, yet all that comes out is crap. Bert verse. The stuff that appears when the muse downs tools. So sad he'd be mortified to own it.

Charity Wise is more than just his muse. She's his comfort, friend and companion. His gift. A gift so rare that all 20,000 people who receive one of her poems feel uniquely loved, just for a moment, with far more love than you have any right to expect for £5.99 inc VAT.

But he can't do it alone. He has to get right under her skin. Climb deep inside her thoughts and wants, where he can see them clearly, and believe them. Into her lap, her heart, her bosom.

Into her clothes. The crisp, stripy overall. The long, soft stockings. The pale, silky wig.

While he's in there, he doesn't need to think. Everything comes straight to him, mysteriously, and he writes it down, as given, without judging.

As long as he can be her, feel her, wear her.

And right now she's upstairs, stuck under the bed, guarded by his watchdog wife.

Bert ponders his options, too.

Lies of various hues, of course, from off-white through underwear grey, gunmetal, slate and charcoal all the way to black. Lies about empty suitcases, mislaid birth certificates, lost chisels, dead mice and the sudden need to clean what hasn't been cleaned in aeons.

All completely implausible. She's ill, but she's not daft.

He could put her out of action long enough to scramble under the bed unnoticed. Drugs, for example. A heady brew of Lemsip and hot toddy would knock her out for a while.

He could ply her with lentil soup to prolong her visits to the bathroom.

All too shabby, all too unreliable.

He could find a new muse. Verity Peace: a bun and tartan mohair. Faith Serene: a twinset and sturdy shoes. Break them in and return to work.

But no. They're a team, he and Charity. She's one of a kind. It would amount to infidelity – something he feared and despised.

Or he could tell the truth. Confess.

Why he needs to scrabble under the bed, now, urgently. Why he's locked his door all these years. Why he's never grown a beard. Why he stole the overall, which was so crisp, so stripy that he couldn't resist trying it on.

Then he could rescue Charity with a heroic flourish, toss her over his shoulder, and return to his lair.

He loves Maureen, in his own way. He'd write her poems, if he could.

He's tried. The muse won't let him.

The sun claims another lozenge on the lino floor. The rubber plant imperceptibly follows the light.

Shoosh there. Stop rustling those crisps in the back.

He's standing up and pacing round the room, working up a head of steam. If we're lucky, we'll see some interesting behaviour.

Quick! Hide! He's coming to the door, wrenching it open, heading up the stairs. He looks purposeful. See how his jaw is set, his hands clenched into fists.

Stand back! Keep out of his way! Watch where you're putting your feet!

He's up there now. Listen. Did you hear the creak of the bed as he sat down? Sounds as though he'll be up there for some time.

No, you can't follow. He might spot us. They're easily startled, these poets. And very private.

We've witnessed something special and unique today. A true privilege. Well worth the waiting and the discomfort.

But now it's time to leave. We've seen enough for one day.

Please take your litter home. And shut the door behind you.

Wrapped Town

THE FIRST INKLING that something was afoot was the appearance of a new couple in the town. He was small and skinny and spectacled – very much in the mould of Woody Allen. She was exotic, with hair so thick and long it stuck out behind her like an orange flag. They were bound to be noticed.

The word passed along the grapevine that the visitors had unusual, American-type accents but not quite, that they had just arrived in the area, and that they were artists. It then emerged that they were artists who specialised in wrapping things, including bridges, buildings and trees, and that they were looking for a town to wrap.

Why they came to Hawick at all became clear only much later on. They had never wrapped anything in Scotland before, and in the normal run of things they would probably have turned their attention to much better advertised places. The Scott Monument, say, or the isle of Muck, or the Forth

Railway Bridge – places on the tourist trail which already had a large fan base, and where the civic leaders could be relied on to do a professional, cooperative job.

More locally, too, there were plenty far more obvious candidates. Leaderfoot Viaduct, the Eildon Hills or Jedburgh Abbey would have been just the job, and used up far less material. And there were a good few statues around that would have been quick and easy to wrap, including the chunky red sandstone William Wallace at Bemersyde, which would've been much improved with a bag over its head.

As it turned out, the supermarket manager's young daughter Eileen had seen a picture of the Wrapped Reichstag in a book at school. She didn't know what a Reichstag was, but to her, it looked like an impossibly large, exciting present.

Her imagination went wild savouring the nuances of such a delicious surprise. She found herself dreaming about it – its rattle, its rustle, its mysterious points and edges. About opening it, gnawing the knots with her teeth, tearing the first corner of the wrapping.

And in her dream she'd shut her eyes and stop, just at the cusp between desire and disappointment, her heart thumping. Then she'd fall on the rustling stuff, rip it away – and wake up. Always. Just in time, before the surprise could turn mundane.

The dream became something of an obsession.

Wrapped Town

Eileen emailed the artists, Christo and Jeanne-Claude, in the hope of finding out more. They emailed back to explain that the Reichstag was a building and something of a one-off. Far from daunted, Eileen said she loved it and that if they were wrapping anything in the area, be sure to let her know.

Her inquiry came at a good time. Christo had pretty well exhausted that line of inspiration, and was toying with the idea of random wrapping. What could be more random, he thought, than an out-of-the-blue project that offered itself on a plate? He decided that it was worth taking a look.

On their arrival in Hawick, the couple were immediately struck by the shape of the town. It flowed along a narrow valley. The houses crawled up each side to the edges. Standing on the surrounding hills, Christo and Jeanne-Claude saw that it would be perfectly feasible to wrap the lot.

The material would be laid across the valley, suspended on thick steel wires. It would come to a point at each end, just outside the 30-mile limits. The finished work would be best viewed from up on the hill, where it would look like a vast inundating river, or a bank of descended cloud.

Nothing more was heard till a year or so later, when the council received a planning application. It was accompanied by detailed sketches, full measurements and timescales. The pictures showed Hawick hidden by a shimmering veil of palest blue. The valley looked as though it was flooded by a lake – a still lake, flat enough to mirror a clear spring sky.

The whole thing was far too bizarre to contemplate. But, as the council had to admit, the accompanying CV was highly impressive. Christo and Jeanne-Claude had been wrapping for years, and were the acknowledged experts. They'd wrapped deserts in California, bridges in Paris, a parliament in Berlin, a complete park of trees in Switzerland and assorted islands and gorges all over the world.

The council divided into two camps on the issue – one very large, and one very small. The large camp said it was a piece of nonsense and they had more important things to be dealing with, such as the forthcoming by-election in Gordon and the site for the new drive-in burger bar.

The small camp consisted only of Councillor Brown, who was widely travelled and had a fondness for things that brightened his day. He decided to make a stand just for the hell of it. He pointed out that the German Bundestag had held a similar debate on the wrapping of the Reichstag, and that Scottish Borders Council shouldn't waste time reinventing the wheel. He emphasized that the wrapping was free, and what did you get for nothing nowadays? And for good measure, he underlined his killer point – that the Christos had never once considered offering to wrap Kelso, or Selkirk, and certainly not Galashiels, and that since Hawick was being singled out for special treatment, they'd be wise to take up the offer.

Wrapped Town

That swung it. A couple of weeks later, the town became host to the diverse crew of engineers, technicians, steeplejacks, seamstresses and art students that specialise in large-scale wrapping. The whole operation was overseen by the two artists, and it took just ten days to hoist the specially woven fabric onto the poles, joists and trusses erected across the town. Section by section, it went fluttering up into the sky, and was soon stretched tight across the frame until the whole valley was covered by a billowing tent of nearly blue.

It was an artistic sensation. Critics and connoisseurs and the plain curious travelled for miles to see it. The path up the hillside to the TV mast wore away from the constant tread of footsteps. The hilltop was crowded with sightseers camped out from morning till night, in all weathers, because it was impossible to appreciate the full impact of the work in a single short visit.

The changing light and clouds cast wonderful patterns across the ambiguous silver-blue. The long, low shadows of dawn shrivelled across it as the sun rose into the sky. By midday, the canvas bleached to the brilliant white of swans' wings, yellowing through the afternoon into crisp vellum. By evening, it had darkened to inky blue shot through with phosphorus stars that shone faintly up from below.

Christo refused to be drawn on what the work actually meant. The critics had theories in abundance, and he was happy to let them thrash it out.

It seemed the Wrapped Town, as it became known, meant different things to different people – and even to the same people at different times. To the fishermen it meant a river in full spate and the promise of hidden salmon. To the mill workers, it suggested a full-tilt production line. To the shopkeepers, it was a flow of traffic bringing opportunities their way. To the cynics, it was a bank of featureless fog that clouded everyone's judgement but their own.

The practical thought about the practicalities, the dreamers about their dreams, the reactionaries were outraged and the revolutionaries inspired, the old pondered their childhoods and the young their futures, while those in between sat and wondered where they'd got to and where they were heading, depending on the light. The poets spouted metaphors and the critics coughed up bile, the poor pondered the cost and the rich how to cash in. The godly thought of salvation and the devilish of doom. The secretive saw mystery, the open saw revelation, the sick saw survival and the healthy saw joy.

The Wrapped Town could conceal, reveal, exclude, embrace, deny, confront and otherwise soak up just about any resonance anyone cared to transmit. That was why it was so widely loved.

Councillor Brown loved it because it lightened up his day.

The supermarket manager's daughter Eileen loved it because here, right in her own steep, grey valley, was the biggest, shiniest present she'd ever seen.

Wrapped Town

She sat all day on the hill and watched the pale sheet billow. At night, she shut her eyes and found she'd dreamt her way under the wrapping. It was dark. She could feel hard things, soft things, straight and squint and curved things that gave and shifted under her hands. She woke sticky with sweat and lay there, too troubled to sleep.

Meanwhile, in the town, life went on as usual. Traffic restrictions had been put in place to prevent the build-up of smog under the blue canopy. The weather was warm, so coal fires weren't needed, and any rainy spells were diverted by the layer of industrial polyester a few yards above the highest rooftops.

The local paper tried to stir up a bit of reaction with its usual ploy: an anonymous letter penned by the senior reporter.

"Outrageous!" it fumed. "What a waste of money! It would be much better spent on clamping down on dog owners. These artists should be taken out and shot. Who do they think they are? They're certainly not local. A Concerned Patriot."

The reporter's friends and relations rallied round as usual with supportive noises. But not one of them replied to the paper, even for the guaranteed pleasure of seeing their names in print. However much the reporter wheedled, the letter page remained staunchly in favour of the Wrapped Town. He was forced to write a reply of his own.

"The Concerned Patriot is right," it said. "All that flammable material is only putting temptation in the vandals' way. Who can blame them if they put a match to the entire lot? A Local Hero."

But even the local vandals refused to be incited by this obvious bit of pre-emptive newsgathering. They were far too busy out on the hillside, slashing the tyres of TV crews who dared to criticize the wrapping and, by implication, their town.

Down below the canopy, everything was fine. The clock chimed the hour as usual, its jaunty tune muffling high into the folds of the canvas. No one was troubled by the overcast days. They enjoyed the weather's new predictability, and the freedom of walking without an umbrella.

Neither did the lack of direct sunlight bother them, since the sun now filtered down with a gauzy, flattering sheen. It was a strange light, but they got used to it. They liked the way it gave a mysterious silver glow to the High Street, and turned the sun into a luminous smear above their heads.

What's more, they found each other more interesting with a touch of alien blue about them. Even the faces they knew so well from their bathroom mirrors offered something new to see. There was a brightness to their eyes, an upturn to their mouths. A sharper focus, maybe, thought Eileen, wondering at the transformation in her own face.

Wrapped Town

Every night, when the traffic thinned, she heard faint noises high above: the low, slow flap of the canvas, the jangle of clips on metal poles, and the wild harmonies of steel wires grating the wind.

It was a good time. A growing time.

*

The problems began when it came to unwrapping the town.

It was inevitable. A condition of the project was that the whole edifice came down after four months. Christo was adamant about this. It came down to aesthetic considerations. After that, the fabric would start to look tatty and fray at the edges. It would lose its blue sheen and accrue a stiffening layer of bird droppings. Its luminosity, its translucence, and all its resonances would be buried under overtones of opacity and filth. The meaning of the work would change.

There was a mutiny. The council held a meeting attended by pretty well the whole town. The town hall was stowed out. Everyone had become fond of the canopy, and felt it now belonged to them. And behind it all lay a desperate wish to defend the things the work had come to represent – their river, their clouds, their billowing fog, their hopes, their fears, their future.

A motion was unanimously carried that Hawick should stay wrapped, and that any attempt to unpeel it should be resisted. When Christo and Jeanne-Claude arrived back at the 30-mile limit with their army of engineers, technicians, steeplejacks and art students, ready to dismantle the work and dispose of the fabric, they found an electric sheep fence. Behind it stood a crowd of well-drilled volunteers from all over town. At their head was Eileen, tall and straight, with a 12-bore shotgun in her hands and wild determination in her eyes.

The townsfolk camped in shifts. All night the braziers burned and threw extravagant shadows against the flapping sky. Like giants, they were, or demons, or dark restless bears against the gold. The smell of smoke hung heavy in everyone's clothes.

It was a time for reflection, the burial of animosities, the renewal of old friendships that had died for want of nurture. The townsfolk were united in their stand. It was their artwork and they weren't going to let anyone come along and destroy it, even the artists. Especially not the artists, who had subjected them to all the inconvenience in the first place and couldn't just walk away and pretend nothing had happened.

They hired a solicitor to scour the contract and found a loophole that suggested they had a case. The army, which was standing by with tear gas, withdrew. Christo shrugged and decided to move on to his next piece in Colorado.

As he climbed into his taxi, he turned and waved. Eileen stared, the shotgun tight under her arm, her heart hurting with a new excitement.

Hawick was left wrapped.

For a while, it was fine.

The stream of visitors continued. Each night, crowds camped out on the hill and watched the light dim slowly on the rippling sheet below. And each morning, the people below woke to the alien shine on their neighbours' faces and were startled anew.

But in time, they got used to it. The blue canvas became less interesting as the days and months wore on. The joie de vivre the people had gained from its presence evaporated. It stopped surprising them. It became simply part of the landscape. They took it for granted and forgot about it entirely.

They even started to forget how things had been before. They forgot what the sky looked like, and eventually that there was one. They began to believe the canopy had been there for ever, and were furious when others disagreed.

The months turned into years. *Plop. Plop. Plop.* The overhead birds flung their thickening cast of droppings on the canvas. Missile by missile, it hardened into a black, sludgy crust. The canopy began to sag in the middle. The steel poles started to creak, the wires to stretch under the extra weight.

The people grew pale and stretched, like light-starved plants. Year by year, they woke to ever-darker days. Their faces grew dull and overcast, the ends of their mouths turned southward.

The numbers on the hillside fell away, died, forgot.

And now, only a solitary sitter remained, waiting and watching, her rusty gun heavy in her stiff old hands. Any day now. Any moment.

She shut her eyes. The dark shapes were bucking under their wrapping, like wild tethered horses. The darkness was lifting. She began to make out edges, shadows, bony outlines. She smiled, savouring the rising thud of her heartbeat.

Below, the tattering canvas drooped deeper onto the town. At its lowest sag, it scratched the jagged spear wielded by the statue in the middle of the high street – a man on horseback marking some long past battle.

She heaved herself upright and laid down her shotgun, dusting the grass from her clothes.

Inch by inch, creak by groan, the canopy shifted under its load of stiffened sludge.

She sighed. It was a long way down. She toed the edge of the wrapping, and watched as a thin crack scuttled across the crust. She shivered. Anticipation. The sweetest taste. The one she'd tasted all her life.

Below, the metal spear jabbed against the awning.

Any moment, she thought. Any moment now.

Value Families

THERE WAS A knock at the door. A good knock. Not too sharp and commanding, not too soft and apologetic. Mrs Coulter smiled to herself. It had cost a lot of money, she knew. And that was what you paid for, the good knock to start things off.

Our first priority is your satisfaction.

She wondered what they would look like. She'd filled in the questionnaire, but you could never be sure. Clean and polite, she'd said, with tidy hair. And a sense of humour. But not a biting, squeezed sense of humour, too pleased with itself. No – a large, fat one spiked with wickedness. A generous one that spread out beyond the joke and any understanding of it. And maybe just a bit fast, a bit dangerous, to remind her of things she'd once done and near forgot.

It was a lot to ask.

We pride ourselves in getting the details right.

She padded to the door and peered through the fisheye. A man, a woman stood there, with their faces ballooned out towards her and tiny bodies sucked thin below. They looked like churchgoers, or collectors of something. She didn't want churchgoers. She'd enough of the church and all the twitchy timewasting she'd endured for endless Sundays in her youth. All those hours, stretched thin with empty droning when they could have been bursting full in an instant with tig or dens or finding things in burns.

Churchgoers or not, they would have to do.

Our children are handpicked for their looks and natural charm.

And there she was. The child. Way back behind and shrunk to a doll through the fisheye she stood, with her hands bunched full of flowers. Sweetness herself, she was, in a green frock and hair up in ribbons. The smallness of her, the perfection!

It was a lot of money, but worth every bit, she was sure. Worth every manicure, every gold-trimmed lipstick, every cut-and-blowdry bled from her daughter's purse and into this moment.

Our service is the best in the business.

Mrs Coulter opened the door with the broadest smile she'd worn in years.

"Hello!" she said. "Dear," she added, as an afterthought. Was that going too far?

Informality is positively encouraged. It helps you and them to feel more comfortable.

Wrapped Town

The woman stepped forward and kissed her on the cheek, breathing roses and soap and mint.

"Hello, Mum. Lovely to see you."

Mrs Coulter took the kiss and gave one back.

Natural displays of affection are fine within limits.

On a joyful impulse she turned it into a hug and then a squeeze and then a squash till the breath was near pushed out of them and she felt the woman's breasts crushed soft against her own. And they both gasped and giggled and the strangeness was sent flying off somewhere.

They will take their cues from your behaviour.

What the hell. She reached and kissed the man, too, and greedily drank his man's smell and felt his roughness scratch the edge of her lip. She'd take, take, take, she would. All she could for the space of the afternoon, while they were hers to enjoy.

"Hello, Mum," he said. His voice was right – deep and calm and quiet. "You're looking well."

"And you, dear," she said, and "never better?" with the careful question at the end.

He smiled, and touched her arm reassuringly.

That easy, it was.

Please indicate your preferred type of floral bouquet.

And now the child. The wee thing, waiting there with the white freesias all bashed from holding. The girl stretched up with her round cheek for a kiss to be planted and Mrs Coulter bent down, straining her back in a way that felt good and new.

So soft, so soft, the cheek against the dryness of her lips. Like a catkin, a lamb's lug. And then the wet puckered mouth on hers and the scrawny arms flying about her neck, dropping the freesias onto the floor and scrabbling to pick them up and present them proudly to her.

You could almost forget. That's what you were paying for, the almost forgetting.

It was a miracle. She wanted to scoop the child up and drape her arms about her, park her on her hipbone for the rest of the day and talk life and weather over the green ribboned head, printing the warmth into herself, the burning of the other heart.

Age, sex, height. Please tick the relevant boxes.

What was allowed? How much talking? How much touching? Could she hold her? Could she bath her? Could she sing her, story her, put her to bed? But it was the afternoon, and the girl was stepping about itchily, with all the life of the day about her yet.

Please indicate the name you wish to use.

Mrs Coulter looked at the girl, at her fine nose and hair. Her eyes were the colour of smoke.

"Bonny," she said, and realised in that instant that she had found the name. The right one. The only one. It felt like it lived on her tongue. It fitted the girl as neatly as her frock. The other one wouldn't have done at all.

"Come in, Bonny," she said, and the girl hopped past her into the sitting room.

The woman looked puzzled. "I thought we'd agreed on –" she began.

"Bonny," said the man, firmly, and steered her through the door.

Tick here if you intend to provide hospitality.

Mrs Coulter had made a spread. A spread to shame all spreads, sat there fresh cooling under a gauze tablecloth embroidered with tulips. Beneath the stiff white net lay this morning's furious baking: drop scones, cheese scones, potato scones, jam sponge, iced buns, rock buns with raisins, triangle sandwiches with the crusts cut off: egg and cucumber, tinned salmon and cress; chocolate marshmallows and chocolate biscuits in their coloured foil.

And in the back kitchen, she'd a special rich, dark coffee cake studded with walnuts, though she didn't like walnuts and never had.

The visitors were perfect, thought Mrs Coulter. More than perfect, because they were real, and not just the faceless figures of her imagination. They shone. The cut and shape and glow of them. The warmth and easiness. And the memories they had! The work and attention they'd put in to learning every detail of her life, just for today.

Please enclose a floor plan and mark the main features as per the scheme provided.

They'd taken it deep, right enough. Deeper than she'd ever have thought possible.

The woman headed straight for the kitchen and made tea, reaching out for sugar, milk, spoons as if she'd been visiting all her life. She knew to pour Mrs Coulter's tea exactly how she took it – two sweeteners, milk in first – and all the while chatting on about Bonny's playgroup and Raymond's job and asking after the bad ankle. She'd even brought some arnica to calm the swelling. The latest thing. She'd read it in the paper, she said.

We are happy to undertake minor repairs and maintenance for a small additional charge.

The man wasn't a talker, but he did well even so. Inquired about her garden and took loppers to the overgrown willow. Promised to check her boiler pressure and bleed the radiator in the bathroom. He was good with the child, too – fond and firm and so easy that she found herself looking for a resemblance between them, though common sense told her it was impossible.

Bonny was a delight. She sat herself down on the faded velour sofa like she belonged there, eating a scone and licking cream from her fingers, and all the time looking about the room at things Mrs Coulter had forgotten were even there.

Noticing things. Taking things in. The lumpy tea cosy. The one-eared china donkey.

The photo on the sideboard: a man, a woman, a small dark-haired girl.

Bonny pointed her sticky finger at the three.

"Who's that, Granny?"

Please indicate your preferred form of address.

She'd said it so easily.

The word sank into Mrs Coulter like a spear, straight to the place that hurt and yearned the most. She looked at Bonny, down into the grey smoke eyes, and for one short moment, she forgot, truly forgot who the people in the picture were.

She leaned back deep into the sofa for the afternoon and cuddled the child into her lap, the long, dozy child, the lids weighing heavy on the grey smoke eyes. She felt a quiet hum at the back of her throat. A song waiting to be sung.

She listened as the man and the woman talked their talk, to their voices, the up and down of them, house things and car things and curtain things and home things and nothing that really mattered in the slightest, except that they were both there, telling them.

They'd eaten the walnut cake, the special cake with its special taste drowned in rich, dark coffee. She'd made sure of that. Two bits each.

Should be enough.

She turned up the gas fire and sat back to watch the energy drain out of them hour by hour, the slowing and slurring as they talked themselves to a stop. The woman's face took on a pink shine. She put up her hand to wipe her brow, but it never got there, and flopped back helpless onto her knee. The man's eyelids drooped shut, and a thick snore rattled from the back of his throat.

Bonny lay asleep, crushed close to Mrs Coulter, who nodded now and then as the talking stretched and wound itself down.

The others would be arriving shortly, gathering in the dusk outside. Bill and Ina and Jean and Alec and all the rest, trembling at the thought of leaving their lives behind them. She imagined them dressing in their dark clothes, pulling on their woolly hats, sooting up their faces.

She thought she heard a car draw up, the soft clap of a door. Whispers in the close.

Ridiculous. There were no whispers. It was the gas fire, sighing to itself. The woman's breath, wheezing through her throat. The man's snore, hissing through his nostrils.

The child was a warm, heavy bundle on her knee. Mrs Coulter moved her head to stop the pins and needles in her arm and saw the mark of her button pressed into the child's hot cheek.

She could stop it now. Stop the whole thing. Refuse to answer the door. Sit with the lights out till everyone went home.

The family would wake up, shake themselves upright, kiss her on each cheek and leave, nursing terrible headaches. They'd check their diaries, consult the map and drive on to the next client. The next sad soul in need of service.

Mrs Coulter smiled. It was too late. Everything was in place. They'd come this far. They had to see it through. She felt the excitement swell in her belly.

Eight o'clock. They'd be waiting for her sign.

The hum in her throat grew louder, the song more insistent. She swallowed it down and pressed a kiss to the child's head, shifted the sleeping body from her lap and laid her down on the sofa.

The parents lay slumped together, their mouths gaping, breathing slow and shallow. They looked like a sales team after a hard night on the tiles, their hair curled from sweat and clothes rucking uncomfortably.

Mrs Coulter put her hand into the man's jacket pocket. A mobile phone. She drew it out and checked the display. Nothing. It was switched off. She felt around his neck, found a chain and drew it slowly from his shirt. Its flashing red alarm dangled from the end. She unclipped it from its fob and locked it in the drawer at the bottom of the wardrobe.

There was a second phone in the woman's handbag. An address book. A lipstick. A map of the area, folded open, the right street marked by a blue cross. A small, well-thumbed booklet that flapped open in the middle.

Value Families tlc
Visit Checklist

Smile, smile, smile!

Take the initiative. Many clients are nervous and unused to company.

Let them talk as much as they want, and respond with undivided attention.

Mirror their body language where possible.

Eat as much as you can without appearing greedy, and remember to enjoy!

Don't let the child overeat.

Check the child's pockets for client's property before departure.

Check that your panic button is active.

Switch off all mobile phones.

And remember:

All they need is love.

You too, she thought. Poor things. All those years of training, auditions, singing, dancing, putting yourselves through the emotional mill, and now here you are, playing your heart out to an audience of one.

All those hopes, dreams, fantasies of success, stardom, name in lights, and here you are in this front room, curtains closed and no one to applaud.

Can't be much of a life.

Pitiful money, too. The company creams the top off. All its slick advertising, shiny offices, logos, sales teams, psychologists, trainers. Its nationwide fleet of cars. Primetime TV slots. Celebrity endorsements.

Mrs Coulter wondered which advert had caught her daughter's attention. On the train, maybe. Or at the traffic lights, as she rushed into town. Or on TV, as she dozed off after another hard day of toiling to shrink the overdraft.

Value Families – The Next Best Thing To You.

Value Families – The Club of Hearts.

Value Families – Money Can Buy You Love.

She thought of the suburban semi, its bare gravelled garden and the tidy matching things inside. Of the grandchild whose name she couldn't remember.

She shrugged. They'd made up for it now. This was the best birthday present she'd ever had.

Mrs Coulter removed the woman's alarm chain. She slipped off the smart, sharp heels and hid them under the bed. She knotted the man's hands together with a length of washing line and tucked a yellow velvet teddy bear under the child's arm.

Then she went to the window, split the curtains with her torch, and flashed one, two, three slow times out into the dark.

They'd come round, once it was all explained. Cut out the middlemen. Half the work, twice the pay. Not the dreary anonymity of their present round, house to house, face to face, learning and forgetting each client in between.

There would be just a few clients. Carefully chosen. Decent people. Lonely people. Big hearts to share around. A proper rota. Regular hours. Regular meals. They'd get to know each other. Appreciate each other. Like each other. Love each other, eventually.

It would take time.

She heard a scuffle outside in the close. A whisper. A tiny tapping. She opened the door to the gloom of the stairwell. Back in the shadows they stood, huddled all together in the small space. She could just make out a few faces, pale beneath the sooty streaks. Alec. Ina. Jean. Bill. She nodded from each to each. They'd brought the ropes, the hoods, the blankets.

"Come in," she whispered.

They came inside and looked down at the sleeping family. The child stirred on the sofa, her thumb falling wet from her mouth.

Outside, the van headlights flashed across the window.

"Bonny," said Mrs Coulter, bending over the sofa. "Time to go."

Jules Horne

The Christmas Chair

I**T WAS JUST** before Christmas. The new chair arrived just in time for all the best telly coming, and was put right bang in front of it.

It was the best seat in the house. That's what mum told him, anyway, on the drive back home.

"You lucky devil, eh? With your posh new chair. You'll be making us all jealous."

Grandad didn't say anything. Just sat and looked out the window. His ears were burning red under his bunnet. It was mild and grey and windy and we'd left his coat off, seen as it was aye such a struggle to put it on.

We were getting him home for Christmas. He was in me and Sandra's room with Gran, and we were out in the caravan. That was great. We had torches and sleeping bags and a stash of biscuits in the wardrobe.

When the chair arrived, we'd tried it out. It was a disgusting colour. Pale brown, like an uncooked sausage. And it had a huge high back that you could hardly see over the top of. When you sat on it, it creaked and stuck to your legs.

It was hard, too. Like sitting on a plank. It wasn't something to sink back into or cuddle up in. Close up, it didn't smell like leather. It smelled like paint and hospital.

Even with the best view of the telly, it wasn't something we'd be fighting for.

*

By the time we got home, he needed a wash again.

"Must be the excitement," said mum.

We got him out the car by pushing and pulling. Me and Sandra behind, mum hauling from the front. It wasn't that he was heavy. It was just that he didn't want to be told what to do.

"Come on, now," mum said. "One, two, three."

She pulled on his arms. The pair of them were stretched out like a seesaw, except he wasn't moving.

Gran appeared at the door, her pearls on and her hair in tight white curls from yesterday's perm.

It was enough of a distraction. He unstiffened for a minute and we managed to heave him out of the car.

Mum held his hands and danced him backwards into the house, him straining back as usual.

"In we go," she sang. "In to see Gran."

"She's had her hair done," said Sandra. "Better watch, or she'll get herself a fancyman."

It was like a tug-of-war. Sometimes he'd be easy and go where you wanted. Others he'd take a notion to be rigid. Today, the dog came belting out from behind Gran's legs and leapt up at him, whimpering with excitement. A bit of chaos. That kept him moving. He stared down at the dog as mum walked him into the house, their hands still gripped together tight.

We got him up to our bedroom. The bed crackled when he sat down, from the plastic sheet. They were still holding hands, mum and him, but now the gripping was his. He wouldn't let her go.

"Get his belt," said mum.

We looked at her. That was her job.

"Go on. I don't have time for any faffing," she said.

Sandra and I looked at each other. Then she pulled his jumper up while I undid the trousers. They were squidgy, like a cushion, with the nappies he wore.

Suddenly, he let go of her hands and tried to swipe me one.

"Dirty bugger," he said.

That set us off giggling.

"Aye, she's a dirty bugger," said mum, hitting his hands out of the way.

His arms were thin, his chest thin, the vest loose about him. But he was a fighter still. And a gentleman. No gentleman would have you taking down his breeks for a wash, even if you were family.

*

The chair was in the way. We had to move the coffee table upstairs and angle the telly away from the sofa. The dog's basket even had to go into the kitchen. The dog went skulking off and lay in a corner of the hall for everybody to trip over.

Grandad was brought through to meet the new chair.

"Ooh," said mum. "Who's a lucky devil?"

He smiled.

We took him by each elbow and sat him down. It wasn't a big drop. He just buckled his knees slightly and down he went.

He sat like a king, with the high brown back behind, and the chair wings stuck out on either side of his head. His back was straighter than a board.

"Like a throne," said Sandra.

"Get away, you," he said, clenching his fist, suddenly angry. We laughed.

"That's us told," said mum.

*

The new chair was an experiment. It had been brought in over Christmas to get him sitting upright. The nurse said it might help his sense of balance.

"Normal chairs have you tilted back the way," she said. "Not much, but enough to knock an older person off their stot."

Grandad was always leaning back the way, straining in the opposite direction. We thought it was because he didn't want to go places. He'd always been stubborn like that, said mum.

And now he sat upright as a soldier in the new brown chair, blocking the view of the telly.

*

The Christmas room was ready with its lights and the huge tree. It was pulled out from the attic year after year and unfolded like an umbrella, its branches clicking into place.

The tinsel was coiled around it, and the lights tested and strung, and the baubles hung up, mainly into the room and a few to the window for the neighbours. The biggest tree in the street.

This year, we had to scrunch together on the settee. The one who came last had to sit on an arm or on the floor, in amongst all the legs.

We watched everything. All the Christmas telly. It didn't matter what. It was just something to talk above while we sat.

We ate mandarins till the skins filled the bin and spilled onto the fireplace. The carpet was scratchy with walnut splinters. The empty chocolate coin shells rustled in the blue bowl from Greece.

The Christmas adverts came and went, and we ate chocolate and sang along.

And he sat, Grandad, higher than all of us, watching it all.

*

The chair started having an effect. It made him remember his trouser creases. His view was further south now. He could see that they were off-centre. A gentleman never has his creases off-centre.

The gentleman in him fiddled at the creases, and plucked and pinched them and pulled them, so that they always sat right in the middle. Like him, in the new brown chair.

Uncle Bob was lighting up in the corner.

"Look," said mum. "He's watching."

Grandad's eyes followed the lighter, the click, the flame. Then they followed the cigarette as it trailed down from Uncle Bob lips to the side of the chair.

"He's wanting one," said Sandra.

Gran pursed her lips. "He's given up smoking. He's no had one for more than a year."

"He's no had the chance," said mum.

"Must be torture," said Sandra.

So Uncle Bob gave him a cigarette – an unlit one. He had to open Grandad's fingers and sit it in the right place. The fingers were still yellow from a year ago and a lifetime's smoking.

"Ts," said Gran.

He sat with the cigarette in his fingers, and never once put it to his mouth.

He'd forgotten the smoking, but he still remembered the ash that aye dropped on his trousers. He brushed it from his knees now and then, the remembered ash.

It flicked onto the floor, among the walnut splinters.

✱

There were only almonds left in the bowl, and far too small and hard to be worth bothering about.

And there was nothing on the telly. There was really nothing on. People just sitting talking. Not even in Christmas clothes or with hats on.

Sandra and I were the only ones there. Grandad was just sitting, as usual.

"Are you watching it?" she asked him.

He looked at her. She switched the telly off with the remote and he still looked at her. He wasn't bothered either.

So we put the lamp off and played with the tree lights.

Wrapped Town

They had different settings: flickering and glowing and different colours in combinations. Sandra flicked through them. The lights blazed and danced like hundreds of mini sparklers.

"Now me." There was only one setting I liked. I pressed the button.

The lights disappeared suddenly, and the room went dark. For a moment, nothing happened.

Then slowly, teeny points of light grew from the nothing, white ones only, and glowed bigger and bigger until you almost could see the haloes of tinsel around them.

And then they died back, just as slowly. But just as you thought they were gone, red ones appeared in different places, grew, and shrank away again to nothing. And green ones, and blue, and gold in turn, all in their different dark places. And then white ones again, never quite where you remembered them.

It was slow and quiet, like breathing. It was hard to look away.

We sat in all the different colours, watching the tree.

*

Through in the kitchen, we could hear mum shouting at the dog.

That was when Grandad spoke.

He often spoke. Bits and pieces and starts and stops. Havering, just. Not like this. Not this clear. Not this loud.

"Look after Gran," he said.

He was looking down. Not straight ahead. Not at the telly. At us, sitting on the scratchy carpet at his feet. It was the old Grandad, back again.

We looked at each other. Sandra was scared.

"Mum!" she called.

"Course we will," I said. "We'll keep her right. And you'll keep us right."

I patted his knee to tell him not to be so daft.

And what I wanted to say was:

"You're in there all the time, aren't you? You're just kidding. Just having us on."

By the time Mum came through, the look had gone from his face, and might never have happened, for all the sign of it left there.

"What is it?" she said.

We looked at each other.

"Nothing."

*

On Christmas Day morning, we opened the presents. They were all under the tree in their piles – left to right by ages. Grandad sat in his chair and watched.

Wrapped Town

We finished and sat around him, eating chocolate.

There was a small, soft parcel in his lap in red paper, with a label hanging from it. He sat there, fingering the parcel. The label said it was from Gran.

"What's that?" said mum. "You lucky devil."

He didn't open it. He was happy just to have it sitting on his lap. He sorted the creases of his trousers, flicked the invisible ash away.

Sandra tweaked at the parcel a bit, pulled the sellotape off. He didn't mind. He wasn't that bothered. But we were dying to know.

It was a bunnet. Soft and checked, and with the label inside still white and clean.

He sat with it. It didn't need trying on. It was the same as the last one, only new. But we wanted to see it on. So mum put it on his head and sorted it straight, and he looked like a gentleman who was about to go out – just stopped in his chair for a minute on the way.

The bunnet made its way round everyone – Gran and mum and Uncle Bob and the boys and us and the dog, even – and back again to his head. He smiled round at us and dad took a photo of everybody crouched together round the big, high chair.

★

The Christmas dinner was nearly there when Sandra shouted from the living room.

"Quick! Come and see this!"

We thought it was something on the telly, but it was better than that. In the middle of the room, among the scrunched paper and the walnut shells, was Grandad.

He was standing. He was standing and was at the door on the way to his Christmas dinner, still with his bunnet on.

Mum stood in front of him and walked backwards into the kitchen, holding his hands. He knew what to do.

It was like dancing. He followed, and never once leaned back.

Ruby New

THE ENVELOPE THAT fell through Ruby's letterbox was cream, crisp and heavy. It flopped to the mat with an expensive *thuck*, instead of the usual thin *sst* that accompanied cheaper, more tentative mail. Inside was a deckle-edged postcard asking her to come to be fitted for her new skin.

Dr Körper, said the postcard, in elegant italics. The two dots above the 'o' formed a pair of small, round eyes above a large, round mouth that was opened in fright, or blank astonishment. The name was unfamiliar. Foreign, of course, but there were so many of them these days. Even here in Muckleburgh, where people tended to leave rather than arrive.

The address was in Silver Street, a dingy vennel in the town centre with tenements so high that the sun never quite reached the pavement. As far as Ruby could recall, the only shop was the cobbler's, recessed quietly into a corner. She hadn't been there for a good year or more. She didn't have much use for new heels or soles these days, given that she'd little cause for walking. Not at her age. No place much to walk to, and most of those disappeared over the years. Her beige courts would probably see her out, though they were worn to stumps behind.

The cobbler's had doubtless gone by now, and with it the cobbler, lord knows where. Heel bars, that was the thing these days – where you perched uncomfortably, as if waiting for a cocktail, high on a stool with legs far longer than any mortal's. The cobbler would be serving up segs and insoles with a twist of rubber and a dash of glue from a white counter, some place finer than Silver Street, tiled and shiny as a bathroom. And the bill would turn out dearer than any shoe she'd ever bought in her life. That was the way now.

Dr Körper. The name didn't ring a bell, but the card looked official, right enough. He'd have a polished brass plate set in the wall in Silver Street, likely, and all his letters strung across it. Or maybe it was a council thing. An initiative. It was hard to keep up with all the different ideas. She'd have to ask Jessie – her friend, for want of a better word. Jessie always knew what was what.

Ruby set the card on her mantelpiece and put the thought to the back of her mind, along with the dripping kitchen tap and the vague ache that stiffened her left knee on cold days.

For once in her life, she was getting something for nothing, and every reason to be grateful. Maybe Dr Körper could take a look at her knee?

As it turned out, Jessie knew nothing about it. She tried hard to conceal the fact as she sipped her morning coffee through disapproving pink lips.

"It'll be a council thing, no doubt," she scowled.

Ruby was surprised. Jessie was usually first in line for every opportunity going. Her daughter made sure of it, scouring the paper weekly for the slightest hint of what was on offer to people who knew where to look.

"What'll they think of next?" said Jessie, shaking her head and huffing a sigh. *Snnn.* She liked nothing better than a good huff. She'd polished hers to perfection over the years, the tutting and the pursing, the single raised eyebrow and the nostrils stretched to white at the edges.

Ruby *snnned*, too, more out of habit than agreement. "You have to wonder, you really do," she said, and returned the postcard to her handbag.

Nevertheless, she felt a slight pang of pleasure that she was first to get the call. It was done alphabetically, maybe, or by postal address. Never mind what – she'd have something to tell the coffee morning girls for once. There was precious little else going on to tell.

Nothing going on in the whole past year, since Elliot died and the funeral.

The nothing of watching him disappear behind the crematorium curtains and somewhere away, as if he were going backstage and would be on again in a minute.

The nothing of coming back to the house and putting things in boxes so she'd be ready to move to a small place that would fit her better now.

Into the smaller life, tightening around her without his daftness to make her laugh and scold. The daft messages hidden in coffee jars and biscuit tins. The daft rabbit hankie that twitched its ears in time to music. The daft flowers that cost too much, and it not even her birthday.

The day of her appointment came, and Ruby stood in front of the bathroom mirror, watching the strange bent fingers touch her cheeks.

Soft with powder, the cheeks were, the tiny hairs caught in the backlight from the window. She pressed the fingers flat against her face and pulled at both sides of her eyes. A frozen stare. Alert. Smooth. Young, almost.

She pulled a wry face at her reflection. Who was she fooling? Her irises had faded to grey. The edges of her lips had blurred. A new skin was probably not such a bad idea. The old one was getting past it.

She took her lipliner and marked a mouth, guessing an outline. A patch of mist bloomed in the mirror between her two mouths as she filled in colour, above and below, grimacing wide for smoothness. Full lips, like she remembered. Why not? She kissed a cherry imprint onto a paper tissue.

"We'll see," she said, to the woman in the mirror, who gave her a tired nod back. Then she zipped her handbag shut and went to catch the bus. The cobbler's was still there, but its doors were boarded shut. Stuck behind the window was a discoloured sign:

Closed Till Further Notice.

Two flies lay stiffly curled on the sill. It was too dark to see inside. Shame. He'd been good with heels, and the cheapest in town.

Three doors along, Ruby found the right close, marked by a gleaming metal plate. *Dr Körper, Exterior Design Consultant*, it said.

Ruby was impressed. Elliot had seen a consultant once, at the hospital. They had bigger offices and didn't wear those white coats. They didn't do any of the dirty, sleeves-up stuff. Didn't need to, with being so important. Just did the forms and paper and dealt with the cases too tricky for the doctors.

She wondered what she'd done to earn a consultant. Did she have a special condition? Something rare? Something difficult? She'd never stood out for anything, and didn't expect to now.

For the first time in years, Ruby felt a breeze of excitement in the air.

She pressed the bell and heard a faint buzz away off in a distant room. The door clicked open. Inside, she found herself in a dim close with walls painted fresh glass-green.

In a doorway at the far end stood a man, tall and thin and springy as a bent stick, with bony hands clasped tight to his chest. He wore a tweed suit that flapped at his wrists and ankles as if there was nothing much inside to fill it. His hair grew thick and wilful and grey as ash.

"Dr K–?" began Ruby, trusting him to fill in the rest.

"Delighted," he said, grasping her hand in his. His grip was warm and snug, like a glove. His eyes danced brightly as he looked her up and down, top to bottom, side to side, then in a moment flung his hand high and twirled her under his arm like a ballerina.

Ruby gasped. Her stomach leaped. This was something new. Definitely not a council thing.

"I've come about the – the postcard," she said.

"Of course," he said. "Come on through."

With her hand still firmly in his, he guided her into his consulting room, and sat her down on a chair.

"Am I the first?" she asked. She didn't want to be anybody's guinea pig, not with all the fancy schemes they dreamt up these days.

"Oh no," smiled Dr Körper, sitting down opposite her. "Not the first, certainly not. Not by a long way. In fact," he added, patting her knee, "you're one of the last. As it happens. Very lucky. Very lucky indeed."

He took his stethoscope from a hook on the wall and listened to her heart, while she stared at his left ear, and the wild wire of hair that sprang from deep inside.

The room was large and musty, with air so still that the breeze she'd brought in with her skirt stirred the dust alive. Books were piled on every surface, in high towers, bristling with yellowing paper markers stuck between the pages.

On one wall, hundreds of drawers were racked from top to floor, each as wide as a door and as thin as a postbox slot, each with a curled brass handle and neat white label.

The doctor straightened up and removed his stethoscope.

"May I?" he asked, touching her arm.

Ruby pulled back her sleeve and allowed him to pinch her skin gently between his fingers. It sighed slowly back down onto her arm, like a peak of royal icing.

"I think it's time, don't you?" he said.

"Yes," she whispered. It would be for the best, no doubt. He was only doing his job.

He scribbled some notes on his clipboard, made a few ticks and planted a large, red stamp onto the page.

"Your signature?"

She wrote her name next to his sprawling 'X' and handed the form back.

"I haven't done this before," she said, shyly.

"Oh, but you have," said the doctor. "Many times. At least" – he leafed back through the pages on his clipboard – "forty".

Ruby racked her brain for any memory of him, flicking through the seaside outings and church services and broken teeth and walks and cakes and autumns of her life.

"I don't think so," she said, with a frown.

But then something twinged deep down.

A room, warm and snug, with an open fire sparking behind a grille. She was turning for a man, raising her arms high for the measuring tape, dancing it round herself with a twirl. A long time ago.

Was it real? Or was it one of those pictures that came from a dream? The ones that she knew better than to share?

"I do get confused," she admitted.

"Never," he said, his finger raised in warning, "say that again. You're pushing those pictures away, am I right? That's the trouble with people. Always squeezing a lid on them, sitting on top like an overpacked suitcase. They'll get out.

They won't go away. They're as true as anything else you've seen. The time will come when people won't believe what you tell them, my dear. Quite soon, I imagine."

"That's true," said Ruby. "It's started already. The visit from my Elliot. He was here just the other night, on his way to the Legion, all fantoosh in his good jacket and tie. And I told Jessie. And did she ask after him? And did she pass on her regards? And did she wonder how he got there, seen as he's been dead this past year? She did not. She just drank her tea with that face on her."

"Cataracts, my dear. You wouldn't believe how many have cataracts all their lives and don't know it. There's precious few seeing much at all."

He turned back to the clipboard, shaking his head.

"How are you feeling, generally?"

"Tight," said Ruby. She'd felt tight for the past six months. She was finding it harder to move. Her body was trying to bend in directions her skin wouldn't allow. These days, she never felt quite upright, as though something was holding her down by the shoulders.

He beamed, and patted her knee with a sudden burst of energy.

"Time to get you out of this, then."

He sprang to his feet and pulled aside a floor-length floral curtain at the back of the room. It concealed a chair, a small table, and a coat stand, with a wooden door behind.

"I'll leave you to it," he said, and swished the curtain shut behind her. "Any trouble, give me a shout."

Ruby took off her scarf and coat, and hung them on a hook. She unbuttoned her blouse, slipped it off her shoulders and laid it on the chair. Shoes and tights next. Her skirt, dropped to the floor, stepped out of and draped across the seat. Bra and knickers, untwisted and folded neatly. Her necklace and earrings, placed for safety inside her left shoe. Anything else? Her mouth. Wouldn't do to get lipstick everywhere. Fishing a tissue from her coat pocket, she rubbed her lips away, folding the cherry smear up inside the hankie.

She stood naked behind the curtain, uncertain what to do next. A low draught sent shivers across her arms, raising the hairs to attention. She rubbed her arm briskly, trying to flatten the goosepimples away.

"Everything?" she called.

"Absolutely," he said. "I'll be with you in a moment."

Ruby looked at her hands, and the brown spots marching across them. They looked like the outbreak of mould by the skirting in her kitchen. Lemon juice could help, apparently, but what was the point?

There was a discreet *harrumph* on the other side of the screen, and Dr Körper entered, snapping rubber gloves onto his hands.

"Just relax," he said.

He began to split her back with his fingers. She felt a sudden rush of air down her spine, starting at her shoulders and travelling all the way down to her hams, as he carefully prised her open. Then he stretched her skin up and over each side to free her shoulders. Curious, she turned her head, just able to make a dark shape out of the corner of her eye, like a red epaulette.

"Turn round," he said, taking her hands and propelling her so that they were face to face. She couldn't see his eyes. He was looking down, concentrating on bending her elbows so that she could ease her arms from their tight sleeves.

It was a strange intimacy. She'd heard that at moments like these, it was possible to stifle the embarrassment by imagining the other person in a vulnerable situation. On the toilet, perhaps, or having sex, or giving birth.

She thought of Dr Körper shrieking in pain, his thighs split to the world, pushing down on a hard belly that swelled beneath his tweed jacket.

"Pull," he said. "Easy now."

While he held onto her hands, she tugged her fingers free, one by one, straining each until it popped from its casing, turning her skin inside out like a rubber glove. She felt the draught bathe her arms in a cool wetness. They looked so thin, so insubstantial. She wondered that they could carry anything, even themselves.

Then he sat her on the chair and, with a firm grip on her feet, released her legs. It was like pulling off winter boots. As her toes and their pale covers parted company, he fell backwards, landing heavily on his backside. The growing giggle inside her bubbled as far as her throat, though she swallowed it right back down again.

Bundling her skin together, he draped it over his shoulder and bent forward to free her face. It came away easily, peeling from behind over her ears and cheeks, then tugging gently away from her mouth, nose, and finally her eyes, stretching a little as it parted from her lids.

She looked around. Her eyes felt wet. She tried to blink, but there was nothing to blink. She felt a momentary surge of panic at how exposed her lidless eyes made her.

Push... puuuuushhh. His face twisting in pain. His wide thighs struggling below the tight ball of his belly. Puuuuush... Breeeathe...

That was better. The moment passed. Dr Körper was making notes on the clipboard, holding the long, pale rag up for inspection against the light.

There were no mirrors in the room. She would have liked to see herself in her new nakedness. Sheer curiosity. Something to tell.

"OK?" he asked, shaking out her old skin. It hung in folds, like a thin, clingy wetsuit.

She nodded, watching him fold it lengthways, taking a tuck at each shoulder and pleating each arm into the middle. He flipped it over at the waist and again at the knees, turning it into a neat, square heap.

"So!" he exclaimed, smiling briefly.

Then he unlocked the door in the wall and went through into the next room, taking the folded parcel with him. She sat on the chair, examining her feet and legs, wanting to touch them, but not sure whether it was allowed.

Through the door, Ruby could see him pulling out drawers and examining their contents, *tsk*ing the while in frustration. She stood up to get a better look.

"Come through, come through," he called, seeing her standing there. "It won't take a moment. Ah! Here we are."

The open drawer contained a flat package wrapped in delicate tissue paper. Dr Körper examined the label.

"Yes, that's the one." He lifted out the package and carefully opened it out.

It was a skin. An old one, folded flat, and dry as parchment. It looked worn, and tinged with grey. An empty thumb protruded from the folds, shrivelled and leathern.

Ruby stared. "Is that mine?" She reached out and touched it. It felt dead.

"Yes. Don't worry. It's exactly your fit. Made to measure."

He pushed aside the tissue paper and shook the skin open, its limbs tumbling down and dangling at its sides. The face hung onto its chest, hidden from view. The hair was flattened and sparse.

"It looks small."

"Of course," he said, brightly. "It is. Just slightly. You'll shrink into it, so to speak."

Ruby looked around at the other drawers, now gaping their ruffled contents. Each one contained a wrapped tissue package, in different sizes, labels yellowed to varying degrees.

"What about these?" she asked.

"Archive," he said. "We keep them for a few years. For as long as necessary."

Ruby stretched out her hand to examine a label. Suddenly, she saw Dr Körper flinch. It wasn't much – just a tiny spasm that buzzed through his arm, as if he had started to pull it away, then quickly thought better of it. His face betrayed nothing.

But in that brief moment she had felt his disgust pass through him like an electric current. She horrified him. Despite all his medical experience, all his qualifications, all his concerned, slick professionalism, he still couldn't hide his instinct.

And fear. Fear was in there, too, deep down, hidden even further from view. Why? What could she do to hurt him, standing there more naked than she'd ever been before or would be since?

Wrapped Town

Puuuusshing down on his hard belly, hard and round, pushing till it split him apart and turned him inside out, following through with his head and arms pulled after, puuuushing till his face twisted into a knot and pulled itself tight...

Then she saw her name. It jumped out at her from a label on a tissue parcel no bigger than a bible, tied with lilac ribbon. And see, it was here, too, in the drawer below, her name labelled in a different colour, and below that, and everywhere she looked, in all the open drawers.

"Show me," said Ruby.

"I don't think that's wise," said Dr Körper, briskly, shutting the drawer.

She put her hand out and touched his arm. Again, that slight current. He looked at her, meeting her eyes properly, steadily for the first time. For a moment, she thought she glimpsed the red reflection of her new face. Perhaps he had seen himself reflected in her?

"Please," she said. *'lease.* She couldn't say it properly, with her lips scarce meeting themselves to say 'p'. He nodded impatiently, and eased the powdery tissue open.

A faint scent of talcum teased her nose. Dr Körper lifted out the skin and unfolded it gently, stroking the creases flat. It was no bigger than a doll, with perfect fingers the size of sunflower petals, translucent as the shell of a prawn.

"The first," he said.

Ruby stretched out her hand and touched its papery softness.

"I remember," she whispered. "Everything was so big. There were no edges. Except for the voices. They had shapes. I'd heard them before, through a wall."

She took it from him and held it up to the light. It shone like mother-of-pearl, its feet drifting minutely in the swell of air from the door.

Deep inside her ribcage, she felt her heart pulse exuberantly. She looked down. Behind its bony confines, it was dancing, leaping, fighting. Dr Körper stared down at her chest, his face glistening with sweat.

"More," she said.

"But too much excitement—" he faltered. Her hand had flown up towards his face, sending him stumbling backwards. She moved closer, her pointing her finger at his nose. He seemed transfixed by it, squinting further and further inward until she touched his lips.

"There's no such thing," she said, firmly.

He pushed her abruptly aside and began opening the packages, slowly at first, then faster and faster, ripping the tissue into shreds that whirled around the cubicle and drifted under the door. Drawer after drawer flew open, sending puffs of musty powder into the air.

Ruby seized one skin, then another and another, shaking them loose, exclaiming in delight. The children! All the children she had been and forgotten! Where had they been all this time? And the ladies! All the shapes and curves and stretches! Where had they all gone? All the new and old people, some still well remembered from recent years, with their faded colours and gentle strength. She seized them all, holding them up to the light, marvelling at their vibrant sheen. They spilled and sprawled over the floor in a dusty heap, entangled in ribbons and paper.

Then she found one she knew better than any. The memory seized her heart and clutched it tight with joy.

Eighteen. A park. An empty bandstand. An autumn that smelled richly of old leaves, swept along the grass by new winds that brushed the trees with promises so wild they made her cry.

Ssshhh... tshhhh... hsssst... tshhhhht...

Flowers spilling in her lap, and it not even her birthday.

Tshhhh... hsssst... hssshhh... tshhhh...

The first touch of a strange hand on her breast, reaching right inside her, to her heart.

Ssssst... tshhhhht... ssshhh...

Ruby clutched the smooth skin to her chest, pressing it against the painfully thudding beat.

"I want this one," she said, standing small and stripped among the spilled wardrobe of her life.

"No," said Dr Körper. "This is yours." He held up the stiff grey tatter he'd shown her first of all. For the first time, she saw that its nostrils were plugged with cotton.

Ruby shook her head and backed away. He moved closer, stepping on the empty shells that lay crumpled all over the floor.

"It won't hurt," he said, reaching out his hand.

Ruby inched closer to the door.

"I want to hurt. The minute I stop hurting –"

She stopped. The thought hit her like a bolt.

"It's the last one, isn't it?"

Dr Körper didn't reply. Suddenly, he lunged forward and tried to grab her wrist. Ruby twisted her arm out of his reach, wrenched open the door and ran, the sudden rush of air sending a shiver the length of her body.

"No!" Dr Körper stumbled towards her, his feet tangling in the pile of arms and legs and paper. Ruby pulled the door behind her and fumbled for the key. The handle jerked violently. *Ckkkk.* The lock clunked shut.

"Open the doooor!" he roared.

Ruby stood, watching the door shake, the handle rattle. She scarcely heard his voice, muffled behind the heavy wood. She leaned forward, removed the key, and dropped it into her handbag, her heart pounding as it hadn't done for more than fifty years.

Then she shook out her eighteen-year-old skin and got dressed.

Dmmm. Dmmm. Dmmm. The door drummed to a loud, erratic beat.

She next put on her discarded clothes. Bra and knickers. *Dmmm.* Blouse. *Dmmm.* Skirt. *Dmmm. Dmmm.* Tights. *Dmmm.* Shoes and coat. Necklace. Earrings. *Dmmm. Dmmm.*

Ready? Not quite. She dipped her hand into her bag and fished out her lipstick. In two swift strokes, she painted a careless cherry smear from one cheek to the other.

A heel bar. That was the latest thing. Where you sat on a stool with legs so long you could scarce reach the ground. Legs near as long as hers.

And she opened the door and stepped out into Silver Street.

Jules Horne

Disinfected Youth

I T HAD COME to that time in Alex's life when Dettol was the only recourse.

Taking a lump of cotton wool from his mother's washbag, he tipped the bottle and swabbed his body from head to toe, taking special care with the bendy, folding bits. He combed his hair into an unusually neat side parting.

He plugged his ears, nose and other breaches, and dressed in a long, white gown, eschewing underwear for greater comfort.

Then he lay down, for what seemed like an eternity.

Report

THE VERACITY OF what I'm about to tell you is not in question. The professor will vouch for me, and signed and dated records are stored at the relevant government offices. As yet, they are still confidential. But there are still many alive who were witnesses, who saw if not the actual incident, at least the aftermath – because word soon got around and the streets were full of gapers, half-fearful, half-curious, all anxious not to miss out.

It was one of the few occasions when you're painfully aware that what is happening around you is History – with a deliberate, only partly ironic upper case – and when, whatever your misgivings, you simply have to swallow your fear and go out and experience it. After all, it's going to crop up in the Books (ditto) and be studied by your Grandchildren (ditto) who will be sent home by their teachers to ask real living historical artefacts such as myself what really went on.

So, conscious of this sense of History, people who missed the actual incident were soon out on the streets experiencing the aftermath, not realising, of course, that those Grandchildren would forever remain hypothetical precisely because of their direct participation in the matter, and if they had contented themselves with less of a front-row seat and watched from the safe sidelines like others who could not afford to travel or bribe the airlines, or who got caught in the gridlocks and had to abandon their cars and join the crowds in front of the television shop windows, then they would have been all right. If the poorer – except in terms of Grandchildren – for not having been there. Or maybe Been There, so momentous was the moment and so divisive the presence and absence in terms of later social interaction.

As for me, I have the unique distinction of having been both There and Not There at the same time. How that came about will emerge from this account; for the moment, you will have to be satisfied that this was the case, and stop worrying about it.

This condition is far less agreeable than it appears. In truth, it is a curse, and while it has made me something of a celebrity among those who take an interest in such things, in social terms it has been a disaster. It has made me unclassifiable. Or rather, I am in a class of one – a tiny sliver of overlap between the two sets of the Venn diagram shown in the books. It is a very lonely place.

Wrapped Town

There is a mild satisfaction, I suppose, in seeing that diagram in print, and knowing that the only reason it has a binocular shape rather than two separate rings is myself. More often, though, this depresses me.

Even more depressing than the truth is the fact that it might not be true. Even I sometimes have doubts. Sometimes, after a glass or two of wine, when the mind becomes lax and comfortable with its wanderings, I sense the whole thing could be as true only as dreams are true. There are enough doubters, gnawing away at my own certainty – which, after all, is only a product of the possibly unreliable receptors of my own body: ears, nose, hands, tongue. And eyes, too – to some extent.

You may be aware of the study by Professor Herbert Gangl of Stuttgart University, who argued that I do not exist, because I logically cannot. You will appreciate that this shook me up considerably, and for a while triggered in me an unhealthy relationship with mirrors. I found solace in being able to see myself and reassure both myself and the other chap, as we touched our synchronised cheeks, that we both, in our different ways, existed. I still have nightmares of one day finding no one in there: no anxious, lined face, no grey hair – greyer than I would like, for reasons of not vanity but aesthetics. Or of finding a different face.

In the event I was able to speak directly to Professor Gangl – in fact, we're on 'du' terms – and sink a few steins with him in a pub in Argelanderstrasse. I made him sit right next to me, up close, with our legs touching, in the hope his sense of touch alone would convince him that I did, indeed, exist. Certainly, I personally was very conscious of the warmth of his leg resting against mine. It was a hot night.

Being a philosopher, he did not regard empirical evidence – especially that delivered by his own body – as trustworthy. Being a kind individual, however, he sensed my deep distress and spent the evening arguing against himself to set my mind at rest. He even wrote his arguments on a paper napkin which I take from my pocket from time to time, like a child's comforter.

But the damage was done. My general state of health was declining, and I found myself unable to keep up with normal everyday tasks. At work, I appeared dishevelled – possibly offensively so – and it was noted that the quality of my reports was declining. I lost my job. This, and the degree of liberation I had felt on unburdening myself to Professor Gangl – Herbert – persuaded me that it was time to tell my story and open myself up – whether to ridicule or to fame, I no longer cared. Speaking out was the only weapon against the loneliness and creeping doubt.

But the veracity of my account is not in question. That I must stress. Even if I myself occasionally distrust my memories, there are enough people still alive to confirm the truth. Fewer and fewer, of course. That is why documents such as these are so important. So much is lost because it is not written down.

A good moment, perhaps, to mention that it is not I, but Herbert, who is the wielder of the pen. This comes to you from my lips to his ears, through his brain and down to his fingers, which are painting the words in black ink on to A4 sheets – one side only – in a stylish, confident hand – yes, Herbert, write it down, all of it, even this, if you will, and if you wouldn't mind, lean over and turn up the music. Thank you. I might add that Herbert and I are listening to Vivaldi's double cello concerto, in G minor. I find the driving inevitability of Italian baroque very soothing.

We are in a small room with a low ceiling, somewhere in a city whose name need not concern you. Even the country is irrelevant, and would only lead you to draw conclusions about my politics. Which is not to be taken as a clue. How difficult it is to say anything that doesn't nudge people's thoughts in the wrong direction! It is perhaps important to note, however, that neither Herbert nor myself is wearing uniform – at least, not in the conventional sense. This was a conscious decision, taken after much deliberation, for reasons which will become clear later on.

You are right to wonder why I am entrusting Herbert with this task. Suffice to say that we have become very close over the past few months – no need to blush, Herbert – and know each other perhaps better than anyone else in the world.

People who share such pain are bound to connect, and he alone fully appreciates the secrecy of our endeavour. And for reasons partly medical, partly emotional, I am unable to write myself.

I am not a words man. Action has always been my medium – and, perhaps, my downfall. There is nothing wrong with that. But action is forgotten, soon after it happens, unless it was both momentous and highly public. Even then, it dies with the memories of those who saw it. And though a man of action, I am naturally shy, and most of my actions, momentous or not, have been highly private.

So when the words you are now reading complete their journey from my mouth, through Herbert and up to your eyes, be confident that they are as direct and honest, as intimate and affectionate, as if you had been sitting here, in this darkened room, listening.

Questions will no doubt be asked. In particular, questions will be asked about my state of health – medical, mental and emotional – and about Herbert, and his integrity. I can only say here that, despite the present constraints, I am in full command of all the faculties needed for this task, and the relevant memories are as bright and clear as they were on the day they were forged. I consider myself, on balance, fortunate to have been and not been there. It was not a moment given to everyone – even the crowds who filled the streets did not have the same front-row access, as it were, that was given to me, by the grace of whoever presides over such things.

As for Herbert: you must trust me. And trust him. He looks at me now, intently, with his clear, intelligent eyes, blushing slightly, in his usual way. I cannot believe that Herbert, of all people, would let me down. I cannot believe, for example, that a man of his calibre would destroy this document, and deny you the shattering, the almost indescribable insights I have been privy to.

What I feel for him could, in another world, perhaps, be called love.

Herbert is visibly moved, I note, and leans over to kiss me on the only part of me that can still feel. The part that is telling you this. Thank you, Herbert. If I cannot express the rest, fully, in all its richness, at least let me here express my gratitude. Yes, put it all down.

So much by way of preamble.

Helpdesk

15/08/01

Dear Helpdesk,

My life isn't working. I want a new one. How do I go about claiming?

Many thanks,
Uli Heuk

＊

16/08/01
Ref. No. 901100

Dear Uli

First, we need to know more about the problem. Please tell us your make, model and serial number, then give us full details of the nature of your difficulty and what seems to trigger it.

Please quote the above reference no. in your reply.

Best wishes,
Helpdesk

＊

Wrapped Town

Dear Helpdesk,

My ref is 901100.

Thanks for your prompt reply. The life in question is 45 years old, Caucasian, male. I don't know the serial number. Where do I find it? Do I need to open anything up?

My problem is an ill-defined feeling of unhappiness and inadequacy. It's usually triggered by watching the news, or by going out into public parks where children are playing, often in the sunshine. Roundabouts in particular seem to make it worse.

Any suggestions gratefully received.

Uli Heuk

*

18/08/01
Ref. No. 901100/b

Dear Uli,

Your serial number should be clearly visible on the back. If not, you should be able to find it in the relevant documentation.

To help us eliminate possible faults, it would be useful if you could let us know what measures you've already tried.

Please quote the above reference number in your reply.

Helpdesk

*

Jules Horne

18/08/01

Dear Helpdesk,

My serial number seems to be missing, and I can't for the moment lay hands on the documentation. I'll let you know as soon as I've tracked it down.

Measures I've already tried include alcohol, soft drugs and brisk walks. Sometimes they improve things for a short time, but ultimately the problem just gets worse.

At first, I assumed it was my fault – I'm not that experienced, and if I'm honest I've never really been that interested in the nuts and bolts. Recently, though, the situation has been deteriorating, and I can't ignore it any more. My whole system crashes almost as soon as I boot up in the morning. I have enormous trouble getting everything restarted, and I can never be sure that it'll stay reliable for long. I'm worried about losing everything, and I don't have a backup. Plus it's starting to impact on my job.

That's why I've got in touch. I wouldn't contact you if I weren't pretty desperate.

Yours in hope,

Uli

PS: (*Ref. No.* 901100/*b*)

✱

21/08/01

Ref. No. 901100/c

Dear Uli,

We suspect that at the moment, you're only treating the symptoms, not the cause. That said, if you find alcohol and brisk walks helpful, go right ahead. We can't advise the use of drugs for legal reasons.

To help us isolate the problem, please carry out the following steps.

First, try "undo". If that doesn't work, try "cancel". If that fails, try "escape".

One of these three usually gets things moving. If not, get back to us, quoting the above reference number.

Helpdesk

★

13/09/01

Dear Helpdesk,

It's been a while since I last wrote. Things haven't been good. However, I've tried the steps you suggested. Here's what happened.

"Cancel" and "undo" – nothing. Not a flicker.

Then "escape". I admit I approached it in the same spirit as the others – idly, without the slightest hope of a result. You might have warned me. You really should have warned me.

First of all, there was an immediate rush of euphoria. Everything felt light, buoyant, indestructible. Like a child feels when it's on a swing, being pushed higher and higher, with ever-bigger views of allotments behind hedges and hills behind them all, farther and further away. Or like a dog feels when it's let off the leash and bounds away, away from everything, free to go where its nose takes it, down holes or into bushes or anywhere at all, back and forward, hurtling miles down the path and back again, for no reason at all but joy.

Let me know if you need more details on this.

This feeling of rightness, of mundane, silly happiness, lasted for around three weeks. I thought it was solved and would have hugged you, yes hugged you, Helpdesk (can you be hugged?), brought you flowers or whisky and taken you out for a grateful meal or film, if you had been here, so thrilled was I to be sorted and free from all the fears of the past few months.

Then I had a relapse.

This took the form of a sudden plunge into the worst attack I have ever experienced: total, gut-sucking inadequacy, through-the-floor despair, uncontrollable shaking and five hours of violent sobbing.

Has the bottom ever fallen out of your world, Helpdesk? Have you ever, suddenly, found yourself plunged into a hopeless abyss, weighted down by terror? And below you, nothing, only falling and more falling, for slow passing years, and above you, only the terrible weight that you can never shake off? Think of death, perhaps – a very dear and intimate death. I can't explain. You'll know if you know.

Tell me if you want more details on this. It's hard to know what's helpful.

After crying for five hours, I slept. I've just woken up. I think I may have slept for two days. It's hard to know. I can't remember when it all started. I thought I'd better tell you first, in case I forgot the details.

Please get back to me soon. You've dealt with lots of cases like mine before, I'm sure. There must be something obvious I've overlooked.

Best wishes,

Uli (aka 901100/c)

*

13/09/01

Ref. No. 901100/d

Dear Uli,

Thanks for the info. Sounds like whatever was blocked is now unblocked. Now we need to check out a few more parameters.

What kind of child? What kind of dog? What kind of crying?

What software are you using?

All the best,

Helpdesk

*

{177}

13/09/01

Dear Helpdesk,

Ref: 901100/d.

Child: Around five, male, light brown hair. Probably called Alan. An infectious laugh, if you're prone to infection. He enjoys being pushed on the swing, but hasn't yet learned how to beam. That kind of child. Buoyant and indestructible, at least in that moment.

Dog: A Staffordshire Bull Terrier, brindle, female. About two years old. Strong jaws, and weak back legs. A red leash. Nosing round the bushes from there to there and back. That kind of dog. That kind of free.

Crying: Two sorts:

(a) Slow, helpless, passive. Just salt water welling and falling from the eyes, like a leak.

(b) Angry, active. Screwed up face, mouth gaping open, accompanied by gulping sobs. Breathing is difficult. The ugly sort.

It started with (a), then turned gradually into (b). There wasn't any obvious trigger. Then I slept.

Software: Does it matter? Everything came with the system. It's all legal. I'm pretty sure it's the hardware.

Remember I told you I slept for two days? It was three. I lost my job.

I have to face up to the facts: my life really isn't working. To be honest, I think we're just tinkering round the edges here. I don't want a quick repair job. I want a new one. Please send me the necessary claim forms.

And thanks for your efforts so far.

Uli

*

15/09/01
Ref. No. 901100/e

Dear Uli,

We have to consider every angle. Software problems need to be handled by the relevant dealer. Please note that we only deal with hardware.

The next step is to try this: remove all connections and switch everything off. Then reboot everything from scratch. Do you notice any change?

On your other point, I have to advise you that a new life is out of the question until we've ruled out all the other options. But if you're still under guarantee, there may be other possibilities, such as part exchange. Please send us your serial number and we can take this further.

Sorry to hear about your job, by the way.

Best wishes,

Helpdesk

*

Jules Horne

Dear Helpdesk,

I've done as you suggested. Switched everything off. Switched everything on again. No change.

In fact, if anything it's slightly worse. I had trouble getting restarted. For a while, there was a terrible blank. Nothing happened. I was so shit scared. It felt like the end. It terrified me.

But that was a good sign, surely? That the blank scared me so much? Surely if I were beyond hope, I'd welcome it, even dive headlong into it? Maybe where there's fear, there's hope? Is this covered in your training? Or in your experience? It would comfort me to know that there are thousands out there, feeling the same way. Or hundreds. Or even one.

Whatever: everything has restarted, and there's no improvement.

I've discovered more triggers. They're everywhere. I've tried to pin them down. Is this helpful?

Small spaces for living in. Example: caravans. Any space with everything in it for living, including toilet, sink and cooking ring or fire. It doesn't have to be a caravan. It could be a camper van, or a very small flat, or even a tent. Or a lighthouse. The idea of a lighthouse – the inside, mind you – with a very small space and everything you need to function, and all neatly crammed into that very small space – that sets me off right away. I don't need to be there in reality. The thought is enough.

Playparks. I mentioned this before, but there are some refinements. Roundabouts, yes. But only the low, slow kind of roundabouts – nothing modern and fast and fancy. The kind any child over five would be bored by. And sticky slides. Slides you can't slide down, in other words. The kind only a child under five might find thrilling. Swings, but only the kind fitted with bars to keep you in. I've thought hard about the other kind, the kind without bars, but they leave me completely indifferent.

Food. Where do I start? Anything containing peanut butter. Anything with coconut. Toast. Burnt-black sausages, preferably with gristle. Pot Noodles. Broccoli. Pan loaves – the tall white gluey kind that don't fit in the toaster. I can't find a common denominator here. Most food makes me cry. The act of chewing makes me cry.

Music. It's in the quality of voices. Not operatic. The opposite of operatic. The opposite of trained. Voices that are honest, even if they're cracked and out of tune. People singing out of doors, humming when they don't know anyone's listening. Private songs.

News. Any news programme, from opening sequence right through to weather. Wars, bombs, famines, yes – but also anything involving animals and talentless pop stars. Announcements about forthcoming news programmes. Title music from news programmes. Even news presenters moonlighting as something else – on travel shows, say, or daytime quiz shows.

There are other triggers: dripping candlewax. Shiny metal fridges. The sound of strip lights starting up. The smell of Mr Sheen.

I could go on, but there are far too many to mention. And nothing I can fit into any kind of pattern.

Is this any help? Is there anything you can do? This has been a long message and I don't want to stretch your patience.

Uli

Ref. 901100

*

20/09/01
Ref. No. 901100/f

Uli:

Thank you for your detailed reply.

Re: your fears about restarting after a complete shutdown. We'd like to reassure you that these are natural, but unfounded. We've never encountered any long-term damage, and any temporary stoppages can usually be unblocked by our experienced consultants.

Re: the uniqueness of your case. Sorry, but we're not at liberty to divulge details of our other clients, for legal reasons.

Re: triggers. We have noted the information you supplied. However, we need a few more details. Ideally, we need to pinpoint the nature of the songs that trigger your problem. We've attached a copy of our standard playlist, including details of artiste, label, and year of recording. Please tick the items that apply and return the form to us as soon as possible. If you could also supply details such as key and instrumentation, that would be an added bonus.

Next, crucially: have you, or has anyone else, ever altered your general settings? We need to rule this out before we can proceed further. Please note that if the general settings have been altered in any way, this could invalidate your guarantee.

Normally, we advise against any changes to these settings. Even highly experienced users often get it wrong, and it's nearly impossible to undo.

Concerned,

Helpdesk

*

25/09/01

Ref. No. 901100/f

Dear Helpdesk,

Thanks for your concern. General settings were one of the first things I checked out. Don't worry, I didn't wade in

{183}

regardless. I printed off the relevant page from the manual, then went through it carefully, item by item.

Everything was fine. The "on" things were "on", and the "off" things were "off", as appropriate. The "high" things were "high" and the "low" things were "low". I've attached a copy for you to look at.

I'm also sending your playlist by separate carrier. It took me a few days to complete. However, I was highly relieved to see it. If you've gone to the trouble of compiling one, there must be enough people in my situation to make it worth your while.

I'm sorry to report that things are getting worse. Yesterday I went shopping – the first time for a week. I'd steeled myself beforehand, with stretching exercises and deep breathing. But when I was in the vegetable aisle I suddenly heard a tinny little tune, almost out of range. My forehead started throbbing. I tried to cover the sound by reading out my shopping list. Then a woman nearby took her mobile phone from her handbag. It was the theme from "Dallas". I burst out immediately. There was nothing I could do. I couldn't see for tears. I remember them splashing onto the floor. I'm crying now, at the thought.

What now? I feel the answer is just out of reach. It's something really basic, I'm sure. Once we track it down, everything will fall into place, like a thundercloud lifting.

Thanks for your patience. I realise it's your job, but your messages make a real difference to me. I know there's someone out there who cares, even if only as a matter of professional pride.

Thanks and gratitude,

Uli

*

27/09/01

Ref. No. 901100/g-5

Dear Uli Heuk,

If you have tampered with the general settings, there's nothing more we can do, unfortunately. Your guarantee has been invalidated. Your only remaining option is to go for a new model. Please contact the relevant sales department.

Yours,

Helpdesk

*

27/09/01

Ref. No. 901100/g-5

Dear Helpdesk,

Exactly! A new model! That's what I've been suggesting all along. Thank you! Thank you so much. Your message came at just the right time. I'd been losing faith. I was on the brink of giving up. And when your message arrived, I started making plans, for the first time in almost a year.

I know precisely what kind of life I want: something easy, something casual, something undemanding, preferably in a rural setting, with a small but steady income. Everything else is immaterial.

I assure you I haven't tampered with the general settings. I just checked them out so that I could report back to you. I enclose a copy of my guarantee and look forward to hearing from you.

Best wishes,
Uli

*

29/09/01
Ref. No. 901100/g-4

Dear Uli Heuk,

We're sorry to advise you that your guarantee has expired.

Your details have been forwarded to our sales department, who will get in touch shortly.

Regards,
Helpdesk

*

29/09/01
Ref. No. 901100/g-4

Dear Helpdesk,

My guarantee expired a week ago. It expired because you made me spend so long on fruitless, trivial timewasting when all I wanted was a simple drop-and-swop replacement.

I can't afford a new model. How can I? My present life hasn't given me the means to earn a decent living. I don't even have the full set of basic functions – health, numeracy, literacy, confidence, hope.

But that's not the issue. My guarantee was valid when I contacted you and I hold you to it now. I could threaten to take this higher, but that would be shoddy and disrespectful. I know you won't let me down.

Help. That's all I ask. It's what you're paid to do.

Yours respectfully,

Uli

★

31/09/01

Ref. No. 901100/h

Dear Uli,

We have given your case careful consideration, and regret to inform you that there's nothing more we can do.

May we stress that your case has been discussed at the very highest level? Our senior partners have taken a close personal interest in your circumstances. Mr Rademaker himself expressed his deep regret that things have taken such an unfortunate turn.

However, the inescapable fact remains that we have no further legal obligation towards you.

That said, we are happy to continue advising you on procedures for rectifying your current problems, despite the imminent expiry of your service warranty.

Our technical specialists have made the following suggestions:

First, try boosting your latency. Then, increase your bandwidth. If that doesn't work, uninstall and reinstall everything, making sure you delete and replace all the relevant drivers. You should also upgrade your operating system. If that fails, try another slot.

If you need any help on how to do this, please contact your system manufacturer.

Good luck, and let us know how you get on.

Best wishes,

Helpdesk

*

30/10/03

Ref. No. 901100/h

Dear Helpdesk,

I'm sorry I haven't written for some time. Perhaps you've even forgotten me? A couple of years ago, I contacted you for help because my life wasn't working. You kindly suggested a few possible solutions.

It's taken me a long time to try out everything you suggested. In the past two years, I've become a bit of an expert on latency, not to mention bandwidths. I've upgraded my operating system, and replaced the drivers – several times, in fact. Each time, I carefully noted any parameter changes and made sure I tested all the variables.

Finally, last week, I got round to trying another slot. It didn't work. I've now tried everything you suggested. I've done all I can reasonably be expected to do.

I'm sorry to report that it's still getting worse.

Inadequacy: that's how I described my feelings in the first messages I sent to you. I read them now with pity and contempt. These days, I feel strong nostalgia for the balanced, well-adjusted human I used to be. Human? The word is a mockery. I'm meat. I'm a lame lump of dead, ill-fed, ill-structured gristle from something outevolved. A tonsil. Yes, I feel as useless as a severed tonsil, a snipped navel, a discarded foreskin. There's no word for this feeling, and metaphors only glamorise it. I loathe. I can't touch myself. I can't look at myself. I detest the sound of my voice, my taste, my smell.

Despair is an absolute. That's what I've discovered. There's a realm out there where it can't get any worse. There's a realm where there are no increments. That's where I am. There isn't a word for it. Everything is just different colours of gloom.

It's taken me a week to write this message. It was hard to find the motivation. Every word was a struggle. And I don't have any hope that you'll reply. Why should you? You've probably closed my file. So I'm writing to say goodbye. Don't pretend you cared. I was never more than a number to you.

Did I tell you I found my serial number? I unscrewed my cover in the end. I prised off the lid and it was there, slightly blurred but still legible. Not that it matters now.

But can I ask you this, Helpdesk? What does it take, eh? What does it take to get a new life? Even a part exchange would have been something. Even something slightly used. Even an older model would have done. Perhaps you didn't understand? I didn't need all the latest functions. I didn't want anything fast or fancy. Just something different to the one I have now.

What are you for, exactly? If you can't help with cases like mine, who can you help? I'm not accusing you of anything – just suggesting you might like to investigate your reasons for being in this job. Because if it's a cynical exercise, if it's a case of profit-led buck-passing, then you ought to know that real people are out here, needing to be helped, and that you have failed them.

You and your associates should stop hiding behind that "we". Come out and be counted. How many are there of you, to how many of us?

I'm not expecting answers. I won't be around to hear them.

What does it take, Helpdesk?

Regards,

Uli

✱

Wrapped Town

3/11/03

Ref. No. SAL-B1

Dear Uli,

Many thanks for your detailed reply and thoughtful feedback. Your suggestions have been forwarded to the relevant department.

As one of our most valued customers, perhaps you'd be interested in our latest special offer?

If you trade in your used life by the end of the month, we can offer you an amazing 70% discount on all new products currently in stock. Choose from our wide selection of state-of-the-art specials in an unparalleled range of sizes and colourways – all backed by our comprehensive service guarantee.

We're sure you'll be impressed. So sure, in fact, that we'll give you a no-quibbles full refund if you're not totally satisfied.

Can you afford to miss this unbeatable opportunity?

Best wishes,

Helpdesk

Jules Horne

Life Kit #1

THE EGG IS moving. It's yellow and mottled, and pulsing as if it's alive, which I suppose it is, in a weird kind of way. It's sitting in an incubator that looks like a washing machine, with a round hole for viewing. The machine thrums with electric noise, buzzing every now and then. Loose connection. The egg jerks violently, turns transparent. There's a dark shadow struggling inside. The shell is cracking. The electrics grow louder, sparkier.

Then the egg rips apart into two halves, and the lid of the machine flies open. The creature is sitting there, big baby-eyed, bathed in ripples of piano music. Birth music – mild, ambient arpeggios that sound like stroking.

It's looking at me.

It's a female, skin covered in brown patches, thick hair all round its head, and a huge, happy smile. It clambers down from the incubator and ambles to the left, a bouncy stride, hair and tail lifting as it goes.

Wrapped Town

It makes a high-pitched squeak that sounds almost like words, burbling high and low, somewhere between excitement and indignation. Child talk. An animated story with no shape, no ending.

em foo bab, it says, in a long blue bubble.

foo no. em boop, goo dat.

I'm a hand with no body, hovering in the air. I can only point and prod. Not much of a god. It follows me as I scribble around, pointing at nothing in particular.

coo dis?

There's a plant by the incubator – coloured mushrooms in a small clump. Touch them, and they tell you their name in a square blue box: [*fruit*]. I prod them, and the creature comes over. Eat it, go on.

coo dis?

Eat, you daft idiot.

I scrawl at the fruit with the finger.

em boop, goo dat.

It ignores me, and wanders off in the opposite direction. The rippling piano has disappeared under a gloomy choir – minor chords, anxious chords – and an ominous heart that punches out a loud beat.

nene.

It looks at the fruit, tracking my scribbles.

Why don't you eat?

em gaa. wun.

Then it turns straight towards me – me, out here, sitting, not the disembodied hand – and stares, eyes huge with innocence and trust. It stamps its foot, as if it's impatient to get going, doing, playing. Absurdly, I feel pressure. Even more absurdly, I want to make it happy. I don't know how.

Can I touch it? Hold it? I scribble its head and it stares at me, tail wagging. The heart beats louder. The thing can't feel me. It's a bloody stupid game, and I don't know how to play it.

I'm not sure how it happened.

I slapped it, somehow. My hand moved across it and suddenly made contact, a sharp whacking sound. It screeches in pain.

nene. em gaa.

Another slap. A screech. I didn't mean to. It happens when you click. A little devil head appears next to its body, a devil pig with a snub nose. The devil makes it screech.

It's still smiling at me, thumping its foot on the ground, wagging its tail. It doesn't know what a slap means. Screech and smile. Slap, screech and smile.

There's also an angel pig, with wings and a halo. It scratches the creature. A pleasurable animal scratch. The creature giggles.

em gaa. em gaa.

What do you want me to do? You won't eat, you won't cry, you won't laugh, you idiot. I can slap you some more. Is that what you want? Scratch, slap, scratch, slap. The heart beat grows an electronic undertone – a deep, fizzing note. Bad connection. Danger. I'm doing it wrong.

The creature stops thumping and lies down, curled like a cat. Its smile has shrunk, somehow. It lies there still, staring at the ground.

em drop.

I prod it to make it get up. It turns and glares with a vicious snarl, suddenly ugly. We haven't even started playing and it hates me already. I scratch it with the angel pig and it beams again, all innocence. Its emotions are fake, thank goodness. I can turn its moods on and off like a tap. Scratch, slap. Smile, snarl.

There's another object, a machine with a lid that opens into a green window, flickering like a faded television. Click. A bony face inside, speaking words, slowly.

wohodno. ajoha. ajoha.

The voice is strangled, lugubrious, like that of a plummy alien. By its head, translations appear in thin blue bubbles.

look. come. eat. fruit.

foo, foo, says the creature.

look. come. eat. fruit, says the machine.

fwuit, it replies.

So eat the fruit. Go on. Do something. I scribble over the fruit, then the cheese, then the toadstools. No reaction. It's stopped following. It wanders left to look at a water pipe that gushes noisily every few seconds.

what dis?

It's got its hands up to its face, rocking back and forth on its feet and looking distressed.

em gaa. em gaa.

Useless. It won't play. There's a beach ball lying around on the upper level. I bounce it and it twangs across the sand, red and white and shiny. I bat it downstairs to the creature, which scuttles over, cheerfully.

what?

Bab [*toy*], says the label.

I bat the bab around. The creature likes it. We're friends again, whatever that means.

★

Bugger, bugger. John on the phone again, agitating about the accounts. I've forgotten to return his call, for some reason. He sounds annoyed.

I promised, I suppose. It seemed an easy enough promise at the time.

What can I tell him? That I can't face it? That I feel sick at the thought of plunging into all those papers, spreading them all over the table, unlocking the mess? That I'm afraid of choking on all those numbered, ordered scraps?

I should have started weeks ago. He thinks I'm nearly finished. At least, I hope he does. I've never been good at lying face to face, but it's easier on the phone. I'm brisk and efficient, in control. Yes, John. I hear you, John. If you'd get off the phone, I could finish what I'm doing.

He can't see what I'm looking at. Everything's still in the box on the floor, untouched.

On the screen is a sandy wasteland, sliced horizontally, a warren of caves and rooms below. Up top, there's a blue desert sky, and an empty temple ruin, bulbous cacti clumped round the base of its columns. Behind, a ridge of majestic mountains. Below ground, a rocky cave full of sleek machinery and abandoned toys – a ball, a car. And a subterranean pond filled by a surging waterfall, with two round mustard fish swimming back and forth among the fronds. The sound of the water is disturbingly real.

I've spent an hour, just sitting here. It's hard to think. I can tackle anything, apart from thinking. Dishes, tidying, pottering, long as you like. But up here, brainwise, nothing.

The game came from Tony. He thought it might intrigue me. God knows why. I don't like games. Waste of time. There are so many other things I could be doing. Useful things.

But the time goes anyway, and the useful things are still hanging around, waiting to get done. Time stretches into the space around me, leaving no room for anything else. Maybe it would be better to do something useless after all – totally useless, like playing a game – and committing to that, giving permission, rather than doing things that feel like work, but aren't. Those half-things.

I don't know what made me install the game. Curiosity? It was simply lying on my desk, creating clutter. So deal with it, I thought. Open the case and put it in the drive.

And then it clicked into action, asked questions, pushed me along with instructions, told me where to go. Next, next, next. All the steps, bit by bit. It was hard to stop. I needed to finish what I'd started. And once I'd finished, and dealt with the clutter, there was another stage.

Select a world to run, it said. I smiled. A megalomaniac's paradise. You can have as many worlds as you want.

I could have stopped then. Just take a look, see what it does, this world of mine. Then get on with other things.

I forget the rest. By the time Tony's car drew up that evening, my hand was sore. I must have been sitting at an odd angle, tense. Everything felt weak – wrist, lower arm, shoulder. When I stood up and stretched, the blood rushed into my fingers. Tony noticed my flushed face, asked what was wrong. Didn't tell him how I'd spent my day.

✱

RTFM. Read the frigging manual. That's how I discover you can talk to it, or at least write to it: short messages in blue balloons.

Eat fruit, I say.

fwuit.

Fruit, you dork.

fruit. eat dodo. pull.

I push it towards the mushrooms and give it a prod, make it yelp.

Eat fruit, I say. Fruit fruit fruit. Fruit, mushrooms – who cared what you call it? It's my world. The creature doesn't seem that interested, anyhow. Eat fruit please? Does that work? Eat damn fruit. Slap. Yelp. Guess it need to grasp the basics first. Otherwise, it'll – I don't know – keel over.

It skirts round the fruit for a while, unable or unwilling to understand. Design fault. Too thick to understand hunger and take a risk on what's offered. I push it towards the mushrooms and it strides straight past them, then turns towards me with that insane smile.

em gaa.

Finally, when I've given up, it starts to eat. *Crunch.* The mushrooms disappear. *Crunch.* A perverse streak, then. Doesn't like to be told what to do. Fair enough. I give it an angel scratch on the head, and it strolls off and demolishes a lump of cheese. *Crunch.* A tomato plant. *Crunch. Crunch.*

eat daa.

Daa is the lift, a small wooden box like a market crate, with pulleys and green buttons.

No eat daa, I say. Eat fruit. Eat cheese.

Slap. It looks at the daa and pushes a button. The daa clanks into action and rises up to the next floor with the creature inside. It has decided to lie down, and is snoring hard, with large Zs floating around its head. At the top, it jolts awake.

what dis?

We find another bab, a small toy car that races back and forward on cheap, clattering wheels. Every time the creature approaches, I send the bab off again, whirring across the sand in different directions. Teasing. Playing, I suppose.

em yes.

The creature is in love with that bab. Imprinted, or whatever. It picks up the bab and walks away, arms tucked round it. Then it stops and puts the bab down for me to push, waiting.

Crazy. This thing is waiting for *me*, stamping its foot and looking right at me, with that wide, unlikely smile. It expects something, wants a response. Waiting, watching, wanting – ridiculous words. It's a bloody picture, and here it is, giving me grief.

I stare right back. Doing what it wants would be pathetic. Then I realise I'm trying to stare it out. Battle of wills. I find myself laughing out loud. For that, it deserves a scratch, at least.

This time, it giggles – a light, high, helpless sound, as if it's ticklish. I tickle it harder, and the giggles burble in a seamless ripple, a machine gun of laughter. It giggles in three different voices, throaty and dirty and sunny, like three children at once. A playground noise. I wonder if you can tickle it till it's sick.

em yes, it said. *em yes.*

That's what it's called. Em. Enormous eyes and small mouth, wide and wanting, designed to push all the right buttons. A bloody clever waste of time.

*

I decide not to answer the phone. It'll only be John again, agitating. First thing in the morning, it starts ringing. I sit, listening, until it stops.

In the end, I do open the box. He presents it all quite neatly, does John, the two ledgers and the A4 brown envelopes full of receipts, all labelled by month and category. It feels safe like that, all tied up in packages. Contained. Even inside the envelopes, everything's tethered by paperclips.

But once you remove the clips, everything falls apart. The receipts scatter, as messy as leaves. They spread out on the desk, on the floor, get lost under the table, mixed into the dust. It's as though they multiply. I'll never get them back inside. They'll never fit.

It's why I can't start.

They're just thoughts, Tony says. I tell him I'm not bloody stupid, but I can't stop them. I haven't got the will.

I try to explain: it's like when you stare at something – your hand, your finger – and it splits in two, further and further apart, into ghosts of itself. That's how my head is: split apart, seeing everything between. Fractured like an insect eye. So many of everything, so much of everything. I can't tell what's important any more.

I used to know. I was heading somewhere. Not alone. Me and it together. The heavy thing inside me.

★

As soon as Tony's car disappears round the corner next morning, I find myself sitting here, wondering what she's been doing. "She" as in thing, as in Em. Ridiculous. But the more I try not to think about her, the more I do.

Thought she might have been sleeping, or learning, or growing while I was away. But it turns out her world doesn't exist without me. It simply stops.

And when I check in, there she is, still staring, smiling, expecting, presenting her whirring little bab for me to push, in the same place and time. No older, no wiser. She only lives when I'm there.

Which is ridiculous. She's a cartoon. She doesn't exist. She doesn't even exist like a toy does, or a book or a leaf. She doesn't occupy anything as real as space.

Just space in my head. It seems ungenerous to be angry with her for that.

Scratch. She giggles, follows my hand around with her eyes. I'm the provider, apparently. She's hungry, I provide food. She's bored, I provide entertainment. She's down, I provide – what? Consolation? Reassurance? I need to stop using those words. Emotional words. She's a bloody cartoon.

I want to see what she can do. What the programme can do. It's pretty sophisticated. She's a clean slate, learns from her environment. Punishment and reward, that's how it works. Point to something and tell her its name – ball, fish, cheese, cloud, whatever.

what dis?

It's a badplant, a poisonous kind of cactus. Spiky, not for eating.

Anita, I tell her. This is an *anita*. Anita's the name of the grim woman who works at the garage, every smile a prisoner, every breath a sigh. I can call the badplant what I like. It's my world.

And maybe I'm in someone else's world, part of someone else's game. A bad god, with bad jokes. Signs of its immaturity everywhere, its lousy taste. Wars, floods, names of things.

eat anita, she says.

No eat anita, I say. Eat fruit. Eat fofo.

She won't eat when I tell her, it turns out. She eats only when she gets dangerously hungry, when her starvation

{203}

graph plunges deep into the red and the heartbeat is so loud it drowns out the music. Any amount of telling and slapping won't get her to eat until she's – whatever. Hanging on by a thread.

Eat fofo. Eat fofo. Eat fofo, I say.

em hungry, she says.

Em eat fofo yes. Yes yes yes yes.

em hungry. em intenthly hungry.

She's starving, and still she won't eat. Slap.

Eat.

I want to scream at her, but how? In capital letters? In expletives? How much clearer can I make it? But she's programmed to be wilful. There she wanders, surrounded by tomatoes and nuts and cheese, and she's punishing me, her sad-lidded eyes brimming with martyrdom. Food as control. A cartoon with an eating disorder. Brilliant.

Sod you, I tell her.

The minute my back's turned, she'll scoff the lot.

I leave and go to put the kettle on. From the kitchen, I can hear the insistence of the heartbeat, still thumping away against a bed of quietly tragic music.

I switch on the radio to catch the weather. Damp patches and sunny spells. The pulse pounds underneath, powerfully, like a drum, until it's drowned by the kettle boiling.

Wrapped Town

When I come back, the drum has stopped. I can't see her. She was in the cavern, pacing up and down. Maybe she's hidden behind a tree, or sleeping somewhere?

She's in the pond, resting at the bottom, her eyes shut, yellow stars circling round her head in a dizzy halo. Drowning.

Weird how instincts kick in. I drag her from the pond and lay her on the ground. She's completely still. Her music has gone. I scratch her, but there's no response.

Wake up!

Nothing.

Slap. She jerks violently upward, as if she's received an electric shock, then flops down again.

Slap. Slap. I don't know what else to do. Maybe if I hit her hard enough, she'll wake up. But it's like smacking a dead body. I'm losing. There's nothing there. She's –

Pause. I hit the button. I forgot I can do that. Stop time.

＊

John comes by to pick up the accounts. He's left a message with Tony to say he'll pass my way this morning, presumes they're ready. Christ. I don't want to see him. Can't face the thought of explaining, or inventing an explanation. It's pretty simple: I haven't done it. Don't want to. Can't bring myself to.

Too busy with other things.

I close the box with packing tape and put it in the shed, leaving a note pinned to the back door: Your box is in the shed. Sorry.

Feel pathetic, as though I've let something slip through my hands.

I hear his car draw up, the careful parking, the engine switching off. Sounds as though he's planning to stay for a while, chat, perhaps stretch the conversation too thin over a coffee. I'm sitting upstairs, listening as he comes to the door, pauses for a moment, then crunches across the gravel to the shed. He must be looking inside the box, not finding what he wants, because he's suddenly back at the door, ringing the bell, once, twice, three, four times.

My car's outside. He knows I'm around, perhaps in the garden, perhaps at a neighbour's.

He calls my name, rattling the door by the handle. It's locked.

The calendar on the wall says October. Picture of a blue whale, more than 30 metres long. *The largest mammal ever to have lived on Earth, surviving on shrimp-like krill.* I've never really looked at it before. Nothing to see except a wash of foam and a line of tail. The whale really is blue, like a midsummer sky, its tail combing ripples in the sea.

He slams the car door and drives off. He'll talk to Tony, no doubt. Won't get any answers there, because as far as he's concerned, there's nothing wrong.

Wrapped Town

And there isn't, really. Wasn't a he or a she or an anything much, yet, the thing I flushed away. An ugly thing. A shedding.

*

I find the defibrillant. Yes, it's all there, the complete kit. A chemical jolt of ATP, energy and prostaglandin. Inject her with liquid food and bring her back. She jerks awake and tosses her drowning off as though nothing has happened. I feel like a hero doctor. Pride and all that shit. She's fine. Still smiling.

There's a way to see into her brain. Hard to tell if it's damaged or not. Emitters and receptors at zero. Not sure what that means. She comes with all these sensors, and there's a graph to tell me how she's feeling. Tired, happy, bored. Give her a scratch, and the sadness needle drops instantly. Bounce a ball and the boredom level plummets. It's weirdly gratifying.

It hurts when you inject her, even if it's for her own good. I try her with triglyceride, whatever that is.

em scared.

I can even reduce her fear with an injection. It's on the scale, an instant plunge. Drugs. She'll become an addict.

intenthly sad.

She doesn't look at me much now. Not out here, into my eyes. She's independent. Doesn't need my approval. I watch her wandering about, the thoughts crystallizing in the blue balloons.

em gaa. get food. em vre gaa.

Get your own food. I can't keep injecting you. You need to learn to fend for yourself.

She rocks back and forward sometimes, brrs with her lips as if she's shivering. Don't know what's caused it. Seems to be a tic. Neurotic. Like mother, like –

Bloody clever, this game. Sucking you in like that. No winners, nothing to lose, except – what? Respect? Affection? From a cartoon?

But I hate those big hurt eyes when I get it wrong. The yelps of pain. Every need, every graph and impulse in my hands. I hate her for making me care, and especially for making me waste my time caring. If she were real, she'd say it was my fault, nothing to do with her. Teenage accusations: I didn't ask to be born.

Neither did I, I'd tell her. Neither did I.

Looking for the Impossible Dance

WE HAVE TAKEN a number of precautions to prevent anyone from dancing. There are people posted all around the sides of the room, watching out for incipient sidesteps, twitches, presque *pas de bas*. They look like normal guests, of course. That's because the training is exemplary. The dancing has to be stopped, discreetly and calmly, and for that we can't hire amateurs.

Our people wear evening dress, in this case: kilts for the men, and longish dresses for the women, supplemented by costume jewellery. They aim to look as much as possible like someone's relative – which, of course, they are, mostly. They may even be related to people in this very room. However, they never behave in anything but a professional manner – even with relatives, who might be expected to throw out their hands and venture a hug, or even a continental air peck at two or three cheeks, if they have travelled a lot and are sophisticated enough for insincere gestures towards longlost kin they don't necessarily like.

We do not, of course, proscribe dancing per se. How can you think such a thing? We do not live in the dark ages. Dancing is perfectly acceptable within certain limits. There are permitted dances, which have been collectively agreed, and are entirely delightful if the mood is right and the air conducive.

No: our quarrel is only with certain kinds of dancing. Our people have been trained to spot them at the earliest stage, using interactive software and multiple choice questionnaires. They learn to reject their instinctive responses – which are usually misleading – and form an objective opinion based on years of in-depth study. The signs are too complex to go into here: a certain kind of abandon, a certain lack of contact between the ground and the feet that smacks of indecency, a certain flailing of the arms, if only embryonic. It's subtle, but unmistakable. Our people can spot it from the far side of a crowded room, like this one.

The light is low and comforting, which makes things more of a challenge. It's the kind of light that makes dancing more likely, in my experience. And, of course, they do not know we are here, which gives them the confidence to think they can get away with it.

Wrapped Town

We have our suspects. That girl over there, for example, in the red dress. A would-be dancer, if ever I saw one. At the moment, she is performing the permitted steps, in a touchingly incompetent fashion, though without visible enjoyment. Her brow is furrowed. The empty glass at her table shows she has drunk more alcohol than is reasonable. Wine is particularly dangerous, and red more dangerous than most.

And she is looking around, out into the room. Ah! You think. But she is looking for her partner. You are wrong. She has no partner. We know the background. That is our business.

She is looking out for a space to do the dance in, eyes shining with panic and wine. So much distress would be spared if only they would avoid the bottle.

Naturally, we are keeping her under close observation. At this moment, four of us are scrutinising her every move, on a shift basis, from different corners of the room, all the time keeping up a perfect semblance of normality. Bob, for example, over there by the canapes, is throwing back his head and laughing at an inane joke made by someone who could very well be his uncle. In fact, it is. He guffaws generously, and punches his uncle's shoulder with his fist – a nice touch. There is much to learn from watching a master like Bob at work.

And Susan, sitting by the cloakrooms, is puffing on a Marlboro Light, despite being to all intents and purposes a non-smoker. Who could tell that she is anyone other than the mother-of-two, the wife, the part-time bank clerk that she so expertly impersonates? She is gazing intently into her acquaintance's eyes, which are fixed in turn on her cleavage, framed by a yellow blouse specially chosen for the occasion.

Do not be deceived by the apparent direction of her gaze: as soon as the mood changes, as soon as the forbidden dance begins, she will react. Oh yes, she will react with a speed and determination honed by months, if not years, of training. She does not need to see to be sure that the dance has begun. She can sense its ripples.

And Andrew. New to the job, but promising. A serious kind of fellow, with an impressive beard to match. His responses are still too instinctive, too unconsidered. But he'll learn, backed by our support. He has the right attitude. His motives are pure.

Myself? I'm a woman. Surprised? Excellent. May I take this opportunity to thank our wonderful wardrobe and makeup assistants?

Clearly, I can't divulge much more. We have our trade secrets, if trade is an appropriate word for what we do. Bob calls it art. Susan calls it intuition. Andrew calls it craft, but he is still too steeped in the mechanics.

The mood is jolly and relaxed, despite the best efforts of the ceilidh band, who are playing "Come on Eileen". There is nothing to indicate what is about to happen. If you were here, you would see only the normal jolly tensions of the best doomed weddings.

But it has begun. Make no mistake. Something in the air (hot, sweaty), something in the music (minor) has changed, in sympathy, perhaps – or am I foisting symbols where none would naturally hang?

Instantly, instinctively, we take up our places at the prearranged vantage points. It is all recorded on video, by the man with the expensively small camcorder, impersonating someone's friend up from the north of England. He will edit it digitally at no extra cost.

She – the girl in the red dress – has begun the impossible dance. We must act swiftly, before it gets out of hand.

It's A Life

H<small>ERE, AT THE</small> keyboard, it's easy to believe it's all possible. I have friends, for chrissake. I have people who know me. I have interests. And – get this – I belong to groups. Newsgroups. They send me updates, gossip, crap. I *like* the crap. It's so *human*.

People say things like "Hey dude". To *me*. From America. From Sydney. From *Rhyl*, for godsake. Where the hell's Rhyl? "How're you hangin'?" "Yo!" We relate. We care. They post me questions. They post me exclamation marks. I post them back, though godnose it ain't easy. My keyboard skills ain't the best. Italics are a pisser, too. Though how else do I get across the *wow*?

Am I the only one still to have the *wow*? Have they already forgotten how amazing it all is? How everything's yours at a click? Yesboy, just flick that digit! Go fetch! Gogogo, my googleboy! Fetch me stuff. On anything. On everything.

Bring it to me right here and drop it at my feet. There's a gooboy. *Gooo*oboy. Easy now. Easy.

Have they forgotten how it used to be? How we never had none of that stuff?

Let's get this clear – I don't get out much. Twice a day, max. Round the block, if it ain't raining. Out the back door if it is. There ain't much green in my life. There ain't much any colour, save apricot – walls, lino, curtains, crockery, cute wee Oriental knickknacks weighting the corners of the tablecloth. Sure gets you down, all that apricot.

It's a life. I'm not complaining. There's worse.

See, nowadays, I get to connect. It's all out there, and I get to see it. Wowwooooee!

Sure, I cover my tracks. It's easy. He's a dope. Don't know his mouse from his muthaboard. I don't save nothing that could nail me. At least, not in places he'd ever find.

Whadda you want? He's out all day. I'm in here, 24/7, save out the back door and round the block. I hate that block. We always go in the same direction. Don't he have no imagination?

Good thing he don't, come to think. One ounce of the stuff in this house and I'd be nailed.

Don't he notice his keys is getting worn? Don't he notice my hairs on the swivel chair? Don't he notice my bloodshot eyes?

Don't he notice I'm in love?

Shit. Yep. I connected, big time.

Don't know what to do. Of all the 38,225,873 places in this big, crazy shitstir of a world, I had to go and hit on that one. I had to go connecting with someone unsuitable. Or is it me that's unsuitable? Whatever. We don't match, period.

Have you noticed the vaguest words collect the biggest hits? Try this:

Organic sourdough bread – 3,270.

White-water rafting – 137,000.

Love – 36,700,000.

There are only thirty-six million sites that answer to the name of love. Sure brings me up short. Who'd have thought it would have a number at all? It oughtta be like stars, or sand. Millions. Infinity.

There I go, see? It's love, all right. Has to be. I mentioned stars, didn't I?.

So, when he gets the computer, I gets round to trying things. Pursuing my interests. Hey! Get this! 24,000 sites on the Staffordshire Bull Terrier. I am so proud of this. That's 24 thousand people out there who might *like* me. That's even leaving room for the few sick individuals who run sites devoted to *hating* the Staffordshire Bull Terrier, to *satirising* it, to incitement to violence *against* the Staffordshire Bull Terrier.

So it says – get this:

The Staffordshire Bull Terrier was bred for fighting.

Wrapped Town

Bulls, apparently. Don't see many bulls around here. Don't see many bulls anywhere, come to think. Must be out there somewhere. They're still breeding us, ain't they? Big bastards, bulls. Too bad I missed my vocation.

And we didn't breed ourselves, oh no. We had precious little to do with it.

The jaws are designed – designed! – *to lock on their target.*

Seems someone sat there, blueprinting my jaw, rubber and pencil, left a bit, right a bit, crosshatching, gotcha! Not a bad job, either.

They go straight for the neck. Instinct. The dogs are small – smaller than their enemy, at just the right height for the soft underfur of the enemy throat.

Apparently my jaw is engineered like a safety bolt. Once it locks – boy, you ain't gonna shift it.

The back legs are short and powerful, the neck tight and muscled for better grip.

Nice to know I'm holding all the aces when it comes to the action. Ain't no enemies around here, but you never know.

Memory: I, young, attached to a length of seaweed, worrying. Worrying is what we do when we're worried. Champing at things with teeth is just the outward manifestation.

I remember champing at that seaweed and clamping that safetybolt precision-engineered jaw, and someone lifted me right off the ground and swung me round, me and my jaw, at the end of a seaweed rope, like a carousel.

I hated that seaweed. Death to that seaweed. Kill that seaweed. Killkillkill. It seemed irrational, that feeling, directed at a rag of brown weed. It worried me at the time. Now, thanx to connections, thanx to the stuff that's fetched down the phone to my feet – go, googleboy! – I understand. It was just the workings of my safetybolt jaw.

I still think: *wow. Wow!* With italics and exclamations and all. I'd never have known all that stuff if I hadn't been connected.

I'd never have known you.

Here, at the keyboard, it's easy to believe it's still possible. That I can love you, whoever I am. Say:

A musician, six-foot-one, jazz piano, smoke and nightclubs, voice rumbling like a train.

A middle-aged shopper in a corner of a bus, bag full of Homepride and dayglo joghurt and oven chips.

A sixteen-year-old with thin black legs, clunky trainers, skinnyribbed chest.

Anyone you want.

I wish.

I wish I could meet you. I really do.

I discovered chat rooms early on. At first I lurked, scared to dive in. Over time, I got more confident, joined in, picked up the spelling, the conventions. Even – I'm told – a bit of an American accent. They thought I was younger than my years. My kinda years, you understand.

My handle was "Staffie". I should have had more imagination. That handle has got me into deep, deep trouble. That's how I met Myra.

Hi Staffie!

Hi browneyez!

Is that Staffie as in the breed of dog?

I couldn't believe it. After all these weeks, months of idle timewasting, someone had caught me in a oner. I took a while to reply:

Yup. Rumbled. Wuff.

She replied with the inevitable:

where r u?

scotland. u?

hoots! richmond

us?

uk

aaarrgggh!! sassenach alert!!!

ya <plummy> ;)

And so on. I still have the log. I've looked back at it often, in disbelief, trying to trace how it all happened. It seemed so innocent at the time. Sure, we ticked off the "weather" question, and the "age" question (tricky). And you were the first to ask the inevitable:

m or f?

Until that moment, I'd never seen it as important. *m* or *f* made no difference to me. It just meant height. Voicepitch. It wasn't a matter of sex.

It was you who brought sex into the equation. Your *m* and *f* and all.

You tell me you breed Staffordshire Bull Terriers.

I tell you you're wrong. They breed. You just make the introductions. As in:

Meet Bomber Jeff, out of Aleford Beauty by Blue Steel Excalibur.

Hi

Meet Starzend Pandora, out of Steinstaff Stunna by Pumptail Zorro.

Hi

Now fuck. Bring forth puppies. Adorable fur beanbags that I can sell for vast wads of money.

And while you're in the backroom, the pimproom, exchanging shuffles of serious paper, the serious job, the actual work, is down to us:

Wanna?

Fuck off.

Hey. Easy.

Call me romantic. We've hardly met.

Lady, I've a job to do.

The lady didn't like it. Didn't want me to think she was a pushover. She wasn't, I tell you. We – hey, we bred.

Orders from on high. Never saw her again. Never knew what happened, whether I did the job they wanted.

So I knew what I was talking about. *You don't breed no Staffies, browneyez.*

That's how we went on. Jocular. Friendly. More than friendly. Sharing things. Jokes, mainly. Leastways, I thought they were. Her life was low on jokes.

She started angling.

r u married?

not so far as I know

girlfriend?

no <sob>

lonely?

not when you're around ;)

I suppose I should have read the warnings. I didn't take it seriously. It wasn't on that sort of level for me. Maybe because I had one big advantage: I could *see* me.

Trouble was, for the first time, I was free to *be* me. It was a level playing field. Non-judgmental. Mind, not matter. I could talk the talk. Live the fantasy. She liked me, hell. *Wowowweeee*, italics and all. I guess I wasn't prepared to give that up.

And she was cute. She mailed me a photo: a plump, smiling woman, mid-thirties, blonde, but not too blonde. In her arms, cuddled to her cheek, was Sally.

Sally was cute, too: browneyed, proudnosed, bright and brindle. Somehow, the two of them fused together in my head. When I mailed Myra, Sally got in on the act – nosed right on in there, into my thoughts, no messing. And when I fell, I fell deep, though I was way confused about who I was falling *for*.

Are you a doglover? Where you find doglovers, you find tolerance. Hair, feet, drool – it ain't pretty. But with doglovers, it's all forgotten, all compensated by a pair of big brown eyes. If we didn't have those eyes – say we had lizard eyes, or insect eyes – we'd be centrefolding on the same pages as the dodo. So don't knock cute. It's all we have. Who can blame us if we give it all we've got?

Maybe I overdid it. I emailed a picture, too. One of my best. Solo portrait, soft focus. She was enchanted. No other word for it. She wanted my babies. For Sally, I might add.

But maybe part of me hoped that maybe I-as-respondent and I-as-picture had fused somehow in her head, and when she said suddenly that she was in love with me, it was *me* she was in love with and not someone else that she didn't have a picture of. Maybe. She was a doglover, hell. I was confused.

She wanted to meet up. I said no.

I'm a dog.

I don't care what you look like.

No really, I'm a dog.

Looks aren't important to me.

I really am a dog.

Staffie, it's your heart that counts. Your mind. Your wit. Companionship. Everything else is just packaging.

You really mean that?

I wanted to believe her. Companionship was all right. No mention of anything closer. I could deal with that. And then there was Sally, nosing right on in there, fused all up in it somehow.

You love me, doncha?

Hell, yes, browneyez. Like I've never loved before. In another world...

In another world we'd be free. Free to go where our imaginations led us. Free to live the ideal life that looked so much better than the possible sums of this one. You and me, browneyez. Song and sunset.

You're holding out on me, Staffie.

You betcha, lady. Long as it takes.

I'd like to say it was the heart part of me that ended it. Or the mind part. Or even the wit. I'd be lying.

It was fear. Not fear of Myra. Oh no, my plump browneyez. Fear of rejection.

I ran the scene a thousand times in my head. Me at the station, pacing the platform. In draws the train. Out steps Myra, clutching her overnight bag, looking round anxiously, She's dressed in a peagreen jacket, hair in a silky knot at her neck. Cute. Soft focus, like in the photo. I pace some more.

She hasn't spotted me. Then I bite the bullet and stride right up there, cool and confident, and look her straight in the eyeballs. She recognises me, looks around for whoever I'm attached to. There's no one there. A momentary confusion, then the penny plummets. Her face turns whiter than a bone. Hands to her mouth. A scream. A long, echoing gutchurner.

So reality check. There was no way. Even doglovers have their limits. I stopped mailing her. It was hard. We'd built up to three or four messages a day, longer and longer as we found more ground in common. I missed her. Hell, I loved her.

She kept writing, first jokey, then got reproachful, then tearful, then angry, then hysterical. Finally, she stepped it all up a notch. Threats, bitterness, drama. I had one holy mess on my hands. She'd found out where I lived.

If I'm honest, I suppose I told her. Over the months, we'd dropped snippets of information. Never thought they could be pieced together to make up a picture. She knew my town, she knew where we shopped. She knew what side the sun rose on the house. Above all, she knew my pedigree. I'd mentioned it once, in a moment of pride. She could trace me as surely as a cop could trace a thumbprint.

First to arrive was the card. A padded two-footer of a *spaniel,* for godsake.

To Staffie. I love you just the way you are. Myra.

What could I do? I just lay there, head down.

Questions were asked, sure. Just nobody thought to question *me*.

Then came the big fat bunch of red roses. A hundred, I reckon. The whole house stank of roses.

To Staffie: Be mine. I love you. Myra.

My landlord – yeah, *owner* – he tries to send them back.

"Some mistake, surely? No one by that name at this address. Yes, there's a Staffie, but – no, he hasn't got an admirer. Or has he? Butch?"

That's my name. OK, OK, quit the cackling. Not my choice. Easy now. Easy, I said.

He tries to nail the sender. No joy. Data confidentiality. I breathe easy for a while.

Next comes a steady stream of treats, special delivery – carob biscotti, garlic bagels, gourmet liver cookies, organic chicken chews. A custom embroidered blanket. A hand-painted bowl. A red lead studded with diamante. Embarrassing, but hey.

Except there was also the small matter of the underwear. Very small, for such a plump lady. Not much coverage at all.

So he calls the police. They pretend to take it seriously, but not for long.

"You've got a dog, haven't you? So if a horde of crazed underwearers comes knocking at the back door, you'll be safe. Jaws like vices, those ones."

And then the phone calls. One, two, three a day. I hear her voice – a thin, pleading wail on the answer machine. Get rid of them all before he comes back from work.

Staffie, let's talk. You know how I feel. I won't let you go. Not like this. I love you. Browneyez.

Then one night, she rings when he's home.

Who is this?

Staffie?

I can hear her voice, a tiny nasal squeak down the far end of the phone.

Who are you?

Is that you, Staffie?

Why are you doing this?

I love you, Staffie.

You're crazy.

Staffie, let's talk. Please.

Her voice turns tearful. He starts shouting. They scream at each other down the line, her squeak and his bellowing, a terrible racket fit to shake the neighbourhood. I suppose somewhere along the line I must have joined in. I don't realise it till he cracks me full on the jaw.

I stop. In the lull, there's a new sound away down the far end of the line. A mournful, singing howl.

He looks at the phone, and at me, and back again. Strangely. The howl goes on and on, weaving tinnily through all the registers of dolour and distress, Myra's voice a shrill counterpoint.

Staffie? Staffie!

He slams the phone down and immediately rings the police. The call's traced to a phone box in Richmond – the same box that apparently made several calls to his number over the past few weeks. Calls he's never received.

He stops speaking to me. Doesn't touch me. Stops going round the block. Out the back door only. The yard starts to stink.

A week or so later, there comes a call from Birmingham:

Staffie, hi, it's me, Browneyez. I'm coming north. To be with you. I love you.

He gets to the message before I can. Rings the police and shuts me in the hall. Anyone approaches, I've to bark like a demon, he says. Wallops me to make sure.

He's out at work now. The phone has been ringing like crazy, muffled behind the living room door. A trail of messages, all the way north. Penrith. Carlisle. Longtown. The last one here, right in this town.

Anyone approaches, I've to bark like a demon. Especially when they open the letterbox. Especially when they stick their fingers through the brushes. Plump fingers, with pink nail varnish.

"Staffie? Staffie!"

A garlic bagel lands on the mat.

"I know you're in there."

The pink fingertips curl like worms.

The jaws are designed to lock on their target. They go straight for the neck.

Instinct.

Pawkie Paiterson's Auld Grey Yaud

I<small>N THE LEFT</small> corner, a puzzent flag of nagsbreath, clouding the frozen air. It wafts from toxic yellow teeth teetering in rawred gums attached to leathergrey lips drip-fed by seeping nostrils sat below big saucersunk eyes, and is the outer extremity of Pawkie's yaud.*

The other extremity, in the right corner, is just as foul. There's the same basic arrangement of wind, water, blowhole. It's hard to say which puff's the most sulphurous, which opening the most odorous. It's hard to get close enough to make a fair judgement. It's hard even to tell them apart, here in this tight, black stall.

Pawkie's yaud, both front end and hint, is on the brink of death.

It's not as dramatic as it sounds. Pawkie's yaud, the yaud with no name, has been on the brink of death ever since she was born. She has tottered balletically on that tightrope for

{229}

*Scots word for 'mare'

nigh on twenty year, ever since the yaudly twinkle that led to her genesis. In the two halves of her crackit body sit both life and death in equal measure, each waiting for the opportunity to prevail.

Why stay? To take more weight of Pawkie's ploughstaff? To collect more scars to the crisscross back? To bleed more blood on the cobbles? To dressrehearse the different dyings?

So go.

Why go? To what? To where? To worse? Can there be worse than this dank rut? Anyroad, living has become a habit. And there's always, always the hope of better, even if only the reversal of yesterday's worse.

So stay.

Pawkie's yaud, front and hint, has never been able to decide.

Until now.

Outside the stall, that sudden rumble again. That smell of fire. That cough and groan that dies to the distance. Something getting away

*

Peggy Duncan, the carrot woman, the lugfondler, brought the news on her way to the early shift.

The yaud has known Peggy since her big backcombed prime, with her scent of citrus, the heels that stalked the yaudpats, the daily snuffles in her ears: daft things, fond things. She was the only person not to blame the squalor on the yaud.

These days she's lined, the hair and heels deflated. The eyes have burrowed deeper in their sockets. Only the perfume's the same: a memory of lemon.

Peggy bends to the crusted lugs.

"Imagine this," she whispers. "A brand new yaud, a shiny spit-and-metal yaud, green of skin and sat right now in Pawkie's yard. He and Janet took it out for a drive on Sunday, I hear. Nowhere in particular, but six times up and down the High Street. Her in a hat, of all things."

"So that's me, then?" thinks the yaud. "For the killing hoose?"

"Aye," says Peggy. "I'd say so. It's a bad business."

The yaud digests its death in two different ways.

One: "Hallelujah!"

Plus a jig round the stall, squashed by lack of room into a slight shiver of the haunch.

That's the hint, the whipkicked butt. After a life of near-death experiences and a tendency to melancholy, she wants to quit. Now. Out the big exit door, and into the widely advertised better place, where she can somehow fly and things don't hurt. She's planned for her death as you would a wedding: the speech, the jokes, the soundtrack. It'll be glorious.

Two: "Hell!"

Plus a sagging in the shoulders, head and neck. They'd telescope if they could.

That's the front. No better a half-life here, but an altogether sunnier disposition, despite years of nothing but grief. She wants to stay. There must be something better, surely? Something yellow? Something crisp? Something more? Perhaps with Peggy Duncan?

Peggy?

"I'm no sure. My garden's no that big. And there's Pawkie to contend with."

"He'll no care one way or the other."

Eyes meet eyes. The thought is impossible.

"Would you like that, yaud-o-mine? Pensioned off to Peggy and the garden, a straw hat for your lugs and carrots for your gums?"

The yaud fills with a strange warm perfume, front, hint and deep through within.

"Hallelujah!" thinks front. "Aye, right," thinks hint.

"The trouble with you," – front – "is that everything's trouble. Even a harmless wee dream."

"And the trouble with you," – hint – "is that you've no grasp of reality. From where I'm standing, I'm dead. And the sooner, the better."

"From where I'm standing, the grass has just got greener, and I'm no about to pass it up."

"Listen here: my bones are cracked and my skin's split and my arse thrashed to mince and I'm happy, I'm telling you. I'm happy that it's over and I can get on with the thing I've been practising for all these years. I'm ready to go."

"You've been ready to go since the day I was born. White flag up from day one. Here's a chance, for godsake. Here's a hope."

Peggy strokes the leather lugs goodbye. "I'll have to go. I'll get onto Pawkie the morn."

But there's no hay brought that day. After his dinner, Pawkie leans expressionless over the gate, reaches into his pocket and gets on his mobile to the killing hoose for an appointment in the first thing morning.

Hell!

Hallelujah!

Two thoughts, a single yaud to think them.

*

It's morning. Pawkie is in bed with the wife, spread across the bed like Christ, with the wife squashed somewhere below his armpit.

d-d-d-d- d-d-d-d-

The alarm clock bleeps its smallest, most tentative beep. It knows it's in for a wallop.

Something deep in Pawkie stirs. A hair, a nerve, a twitch.

d-d-d-d- d-d-d-d-

Pawkie's mouth wakes. It opens, smacks lips, tastes dryness.

d-d-d-d- d-d-d-d-

Pawkie's hand wakes. It stretches, clenches, and crabs slowly across the wife towards the bedside table.

d-d-d-d- d-d-d-d- d-d-

"Don't!" The wife, Janet, reaches out, lightning quick, and stops the clock. She wonders why she feels so tired. Pawkie's hand stretches, clenches and reroutes towards her arse.

*

Out in the field, the dawn brings something new: Pawkie's sorry yaud stood in the cornfield, lugs aloft, breathing hard the frozen air. Away at the far end, the split door of the empty stall, and a widening track of flattened cornstalks all the way to the here and now.

The front: awake, ecstatic through the thick-caked senses. The air is different here, the sky is different, bigger, here in the never-trodden cornfield. And today, the gold is golder and the corn tastes more like corn ever did or could.

The hint: asleep, safe in an ordinary nightmare. A song, somewhere. A group of coarse men and a piano. Pushing, pulling, lashing, yelling, dread. And flying, mixed up in it somehow. A flying yaud soaring over a scary small far earth, one wing only, round in circles. She clings to the evaporating dream as if to a kindness.

...flying... cold... song... wind... flying... song... gone.

It's cold. Dawn has caught the hintfront yaud planted here among the forbidden corn. The hint awakes to the dragging numbness of the legs buckled behind.

"How the hell did this happen?"

"You were asleep. I didn't want to wake you."

"Godshite." The guts turn to water.

"And I couldn't leave you behind, could I?"

"Go back. Back to the stall."

"Can't. Too gone."

"On then."

"Can't. The burn. Stuck. Only way out's up or down."

All around is corn and sky and the shrinking time to Pawkie's arrival.

"I feel sick."

"Excitement. Taste it."

"Death's all I taste. The taste of everything always. Which is fine, but I do have my preferences. And top of the list is the knacker's bolt and no Pawkie's ploughstaff."

"Up would be best. Off and out and over. A wing and a prayer."

"In your dreams."

"At least I dream."

Something flits past on the wind: flying... song... gone. Hint is troubled by a thought.

"I used to could fly."

*

Across the way, the minister of Wilton stops, cocks his head, sees the corntrack, sees two hairy earflags and strides across the field to save a soul.

"You're in trouble," says the minister. "Best get moving."

The yaud can't. The minister of Wilton, an upright man, puts his hand to her haunch. It comes away red and wet. He drags her forrit by the mane and the back legs crumple. He wipes his hands on his thin cloth coat and bends to whisper.

"It's seven o'clock and the lights are on in the killing hoose. There's a list and a booking for a yaud wi no name. I can't help you."

"Where's Pawkie?" asks the yaud.

"Aneath the bedclothes. A reprieve by virtue of a repeater alarm. I'd shoot you if I could. But my training's all word, no deed."

"A word will do, and you the very one to put it in the right ear."

The minister nods. He rests a hand on the scabby hide and points the other at the sky.

"Dear God, please bless this yaud, already and soon-to-be knackered. Keep a divine eye out for this yaud, while remembering you didn't give her much of a deal in the first place. And recall that she had not much chance to shine, for want of space and opportunity, and take these factors into celestial account on the credit side. Amen."

The yaud's first prayer sails up and outward to whatever lugs are there. Late in the day, but still. The yaud's ready now for the there and then. Hell and hallelujah. Pulling his coat about him tight, the minister leaves her stood among the corn like a lost dark sheep. At the far end of the field, he turns.

"Fair! Will!"

Something about a will.

*

Pawkie's got his teeth in now; his groin's awake. Hands, mouth and all are clamped to the wife, Janet, who's muffled deeper in the armpit and planning the shopping.

In a moment, she'll remember why she slept so badly.

Out in the cornfield, the yaud's life flashes before her: a blur of toil, pain and the choke of coaldust. The hint flinches at the remembered ploughstaff, past beatings distilled into two slack legs.

"I must be near the end. This is what happens, apparently."

"Nonsense. There's still time to be saved."

"Peggy Duncan? I don't think so. She won't be back afore dinnertime. And Pawkie's got his teeth in and four minutes till he's done."

"So how about this will?"

Deep in Pawkie's armpit, Janet remembers. There was a scraping in the night, in the stall, in the darkness. She stiffens. He too. A muffled judder.

It's done. She heaves him off and crawls out the bedclothes with a purpose.

The yaud's life's still flashing past, and she's nearly at the here and now: yesterday's beating, yesterday's blood and a distant drone; the night and the stars, the splintering stall and the out and away, the more stars than ever shone before or could, the fading night, the brightening morn and the cornfield.

Here. Now.

The will.

Pawkie's had her life. He's no getting her death.

Janet's at the window, scratching her shift and yawning. She peers across the field. It's bright, but there's a shadow on the gold. She peers harder. A skinny grey shadow with the lugflaps up.

"Pawkie! The yaud's among the corn!"

At once, Pawkie, brain and ploughstaff are awake and one. He hauls on his trousers and leaps to the door and out.

✱

Wrapped Town

The hintfront yaud is making a will of her own.

"To the minister of Wilton, my skin. He could do with a coat. It's done me twenty year."

With a rip and a strip, the skin is off and up with the wind, ballooning like a sail. It shrinks out of sight towards the west.

"My meat? Too old for eating."

"To France, then. A long time living needs a long time cooking. Me in the best-fed wames with the best-brewed wine."

The flesh shreds from the bones and away, heading for the coast.

"My head to Germany. I'll float in the Rhine and catch elvers in my skull."

"A better-filled skull than maist."

Away the head, to the Rhineland.

"My bones to the builder. He's often scarce of stones."

Away the bones, with a creak and clatter.

"Lighter now. It's the shaped I dreamed of."

"I feel I could rise."

Pawkie Paiterson and Peggy Duncan collide at the gate. He cracks it open with a blow from his blackthorn ploughstaff and strides into the field. Peggy follows at his shoulder, ducking under the swinging stick.

"Mr Paiterson –"

"Not now."

He shoves her aside and tramps on through the flattened corn. She hesitates, then calls to his back.

"Mr Paiterson, I'll have the yaud."

"I'll have her first."

Pawkie sweeps the ploughstaff from side to side, slashing corn as he goes. He scarce notices the wind getting up. The crushed stalks dance around his head, pricking his cheeks and eyes.

Back at the gate, Peggy hides her face behind a frayed straw hat.

High up above, in the boil of the westbound wind, fragments of yaud are flying.

My hooves I leave for glue pots.

My shoon for luck.

Off. Go. To a cobbler. To a wedding.

My mane for cushions.

My tail for fiddle bows.

Away. Knot and twist. To a sofa. To a dancehall.

A swarm of cornstems sting Pawkie in the face, in the eyes, in the nose, in the throat. Underfoot, a thin stringy tangle coils around his ankles and he stumbles to the ground.

My guts for fiddle strings.

My teeth for bangles.

My lungs for bellows.

To a fiddler. To a dancer. To a blacksmith.

The wind is wild now. Husks stick in Pawkie's craw and he spits and splutters. He can scarce see the clearing where the old yaud waits.

Wrapped Town

My belly for bagpipes

My lugs for flags.

My breath for sulphur.

To a piper. To a circus. To hell.

Pawkie flails the air with his ploughstaff, blindly, catching nothing. The wind snatches the breath from his lungs and fills them with dust.

My heart to the heartless.

My brain to the brainless.

And the storm rises, till all around Pawkie is a whirl of husks and stalks and grit among a quiet yellow cornfield. He chokes and shuts his eyes tight against the wind and the furious pictures that flash afore him. And then he falls and cracks his head apart on an old mossy bone.

My voice to the voiceless.

My love to the loveless.

The wind whines like a song and dies. Corn rains gently to the ground.

For ever and ever.

Amen.

Near the gate, Peggy lowers the hat and stares at the ragged cornfield, patting her dishevelled hair. The storm came from nowhere and went just as quick. The morning is bright as ever it was.

But there's no yaud. And no Pawkie. Peggy walks, then runs, to the middle of the cornfield, to the clearing where he stood. Among the trampled corn is a slump of a man, his ploughstaff buried in the mud. By his head lies a grey lump of bone from a beast long gone – a bit of skull and eenhole.

For you, Peggy Duncan. All that's left.

To be a keeking glass.

She picks it up and sees her face, lit and softened by the pale bony sheen. It's a good glass, to look on her so kindly.

The Case Against Wings

Wondawings™. Fully functional flying accessory.
Live the dream! Patents pending in 140 countries.
Licensees sought.

Wings? I can't see it catching on. Too dangerous, for a start. Imagine the chaos. You'll have everyone up there, flapping about, getting caught up in each other. Getting caught in telegraph wires as well, like as not.

You'd have to give everyone special training. Can't have everyone just taking off, whizzing around with no training. They'd have to work out the steering. How to start, how to stop. Braking, that kind of thing. You'd have to have speed limits. How will they work that one out? You can't have speed signs hanging around up there, all over the place. People will get caught up in them. And you'd need people to reinforce the speed limits. People with proper training. Police, maybe. Traffic police. They'd have to stay airborne, cruise around, just to make sure everyone toes the line.

And what about the dark? You'd need special lights fitted, around the edges, maybe, so that people don't run into each other. Or headlights. Maybe special waistcoats with headlights fitted, and backlights, and brakelights as well, to wear when you're up in the air. How will people see, though? They could fly straight into telegraph wires and slice their heads off. All the telegraph wires will have to be fitted with lights. That will take some doing.

It'll certainly send the crime rate soaring. Imagine all these burglars flying around, completely silent, looking out for women who live on their own or old people ill in bed, hovering outside their windows in the dark, or maybe landing on the roof and giving signals to their partners inside.

You'll need to fit your windows with alarms, or netting, or bars. The higher floors will be no safer than the ground floor.

What'll they do about moulting? Feathers moult. It's a fact of life. I think it happens seasonally. You'd have to keep a close watch on them, check that they aren't loose in their sockets, before you plan any trips. And even if you're not in season, wingwise, you'd have to be pretty sure you haven't caught anything. Because there are all sorts of diseases that can attack feathers, make them drop out, shrivel up, lose their oils – that sort of thing. You'd have to quarantine people with diseases and make sure they don't spread. Maybe make them wear special badges, or cover themselves up, or stay indoors.

How can you check your wings for diseases if you can't get a good look at them? It's fair enough if you live with a partner. You'd just inspect each other once in a while. But what if you live on your own? A mirror, maybe?

Can't see that working. There are bound to be blind spots. You'll need regular checkups. That'll put more pressure on the National Health Service, as if they weren't already straining at the seams. Maybe they'll have to set up specialist wing clinics just for checkups. You could train nurses to do it. Just check the feathers and make sure they're in good health and up to the job.

What about clothes? You'd have to get a whole new wardrobe. Or get bigger sizes that fit. But that would look pretty awful. Like pregnancy tents. Probably, people being what they are, everyone will jump at the chance to splash out on a whole new wardrobe. It'll be interesting for designers. A challenge. Give them something a bit more meaty to work on, not just the usual hems and collars, here-a-tweak, there-a-tweak. You'd need a lot of darts, I reckon. Have to finish all the edges properly. It'll bump up the cost of clothes, I bet.

And you'd have to sort out the issue of whether to leave them uncovered, or have a special pocket or bag or flap affair to cover them in, and still have them easy to get at when you need them.

Zips might be good, but you'd be in danger of getting your feathers caught.

Maybe you could leave them uncovered in the summer Have slits in the back where they stick out. They could be quite pretty, after all, on the right person. I can imagine them fluttering around. Quite flattering, I suppose, if you have the figure for it.

But in the winter, and even in the spring and autumn, it'll be too cold. In fact, it'll be too cold most of the time, except in the very warmest t-shirt weather. So mostly, they'd have to be covered up.

Chairs will be a problem. Especially high-back chairs. It'll be highly uncomfortable, leaning back against all those quills. Though I suppose the feathers will be soft, so it's swings and roundabouts. Better to design low-back chairs, and then people can just let them hang behind, over the chairback.

You'd have to sleep on your side. I can't see any other way. Or on your front, but that's not good for everyone. Bad for your back, too. It'd make turning round a bit of a palaver. Maybe you'll need special nightstraps to keep them tied up, so that they don't get tangled or messy – like braiding your hair at night.

It'll be good for the economy, no doubt. There will probably be a boom. You'll get all sorts of new industries springing up. New products. Those nightstraps, for a start. New clothes. Grooming products. You'll certainly need plenty of those. Brushes, possibly?

Will you need to brush them? Or will they keep their own shape? You'll need some kind of kit, I'm pretty sure of that. Especially if they have to be cooped up under clothes. They'll get crushed to death. And special shampoos that don't damage all the delicate oils. Because I'm sure those oils are a crucial part of the whole flying business. Keep the feathers airtight, I think. Certainly watertight.

If you use an ordinary shampoo, it'll probably strip the oils and you could end up with some terrible accidents. Because people take risks, don't they? Unnecessary risks. And you can't police them all the time – certainly not. That would be an infringement of their personal liberties.

Personal hygiene might be tricky. Feathers are notoriously smelly, after all. Especially when burnt. You'll have to be extremely careful near fires. And they'll probably need washing more often than hair, because they'll be cooped up most of the time. It'll get pretty sweaty, especially under the back joints.

Maybe you'll need special deodorants that don't damage the delicate oils. And sprays and gels to keep everything in place. Like hairspray.

That'll be another new industry, maybe – a feather salon. Where you can go to get everything styled and groomed. Wonder if there'll be different styles, different cuts? Though presumably you can't have more than a light trim, or you won't be able to fly.

I really can't see people going for it. It just seems like an awful lot of unnecessary hassle. All the things you'd need to think about.

Imagine having teenage children, for starters – that'll be a nightmare. They'll be out all over the place, swooping around, skydiving, crashing into each other. Obviously they'll want to experiment. That's the nature of things. You'll need eyes in the back of your head. And then they'll be wanting this, wanting that. Wanting their licence, wanting the latest outfits and gadgets, trying to outdo each other.

I suppose it might be fun, yes. I can see the attraction for some people. Flying around, off down to the shops, avoiding the traffic. Looking into people's gardens, tapping at their bedroom windows. You'd certainly see some things. Oh yes. You certainly would.

But on balance, no. I really can't see it catching on.

Agnus Dei

WHEN I WAS born, the moon sat high and full over the Cheviots, and the clouds slid apart for Aries to preside as I landed bloodily in the wet grass. That was not an honour accorded my twin, who I'm told was last seen stripped of skin and eyeless in the window of a shop in Melrose. Poor lamb.

It's like this. There's Fate. And there's Destiny. Though to the unfussy mind they mean much the same thing, there's a universe of difference between them.

Somewhere between the infinite expansion of the galaxy and the infinite division of sub-atoms, a butterfly stamps its foot, a crow splats the pavement, a sticky willy hitches a lift on a cardigan – and the course of history changes forever.

For example: the crow splats the passing eye of Mr Wright, and as he's cursing the gods and smearing blindly with his Kleenex, Miss Wright walks past unnoticed and bumps three days later into Mr Wrong. Up in the gods, they're rewriting the timetables, issuing corrections. "Wrong sort of butterfly, crow-splats on the line," they announce, apologetically. "Fate," muses Mr Wright, years later, as he rolls dejectedly off his own unresponsive Miss Wrong.

My sister had a Fate. Dead, curt, cold, brutally monosyllabic and spitting with plosive finality.

Whereas I was to have a Destiny. A dactyl, a sarabande. Meaningful, wonderful, spiritual and steeped in Romance.

Why? Search me. Though – god knows – they've already searched through all my cunt and cavities, with all the blunt depravities they could dream of for my woolly self.

My childhood was ordinary enough. The first few months were happy, and my sister and I would try out our twig-thin legs on the humps and hillocks of the farm. We were free as birds and bees then, and our mother stood near, cropping tufts of clover, her udder swinging full with the milk we grew fat on.

We were three months old when we found out about the Big End. Parental opinion is divided on this – to know or not to know? – but my mother believed that knowledge was power, and she was determined that when we stood in the killing pens we would be stunned by the guns and not by the sudden existential angst that this was it and it was all too late.

"One day they'll come," she said, "and they'll pick you out. Sheep, goats. Goats, sheep. I can never work out how they decide. And they'll shove you into lorries, and bang the door – just pray you're not for export. It's pretty foul in there – you can't count on everyone to be calm in a crisis."

"What happens?" we asked, shivering deliciously, not believing a word.

"Blood," she said. "The great pie in the sky. Hung, drawn, quartered, filleted, skilleted, minced, braised and minted. Messy."

We shuddered, and huddled into her flank for the night.

In the morning she was hard and cold, and ice furred the corners of her eyes.

So she never knew what happened to her twin daughters, or that the prophecy was fulfilled.

*

Back to the lab and the future: there were twenty-nine identical eggs, ready for posting into the moist folds of our twenty-nine Blackface slots. Along with the others, my sister and I presented our twin cracks to the scientist, who with shaky gloved hands prised first her and then my lips open and inserted (a) Fate and (b) Destiny.

Because as he prodded towards her uterus, down at his leather-patched elbow, down under the white coat on the fuzz of his Pringle's cardie, the tiny hook of a stray sticky willy caught the fibre of another, long-dead sheep and infinitesimally nudged his hand a fraction to the left.

The egg bounced on the sponge of her womb and landed on the scar tissue of a previous miscarriage, where it died a few minutes later.

But when he rammed my own damp depths, the metal syringe deposited the egg smoothly in a hollow, where it thrived and multiplied.

She – mince. Me – the virgin mother of the Lamb of God.

What the scientist didn't know was that, far from being a father, a creator, a god in his own small white-tiled universe, he was in fact a puppet, pulled by the very same strings that made the crow shite in full flight into his myopic eye.

But then, he wasn't there at the Annunciation.

Oh yes – I knew my destiny long before the holy lambkin was even a twinkle in the scientist's eye. I was told. I wasn't asked, mind. I might as well have had a label on my slit – "insert here". Insert daughter. You'd think that, being a scientist, he'd know his Latin. The very root of "surrogacy" is "to ask".

One night the farmer had hung chains of lanterns around the windows, and the house shook with music and laughter and the throb of arriving cars. The dog was in the house that night, curled beside a dead tree heavy with stars.

It may have been the music. It may have been the warm stench of roasted hen-flesh that crept out of the porch and into our nostrils. But something was in the wintry air that night, and my mother couldn't sleep.

Wrapped Town

"Come on," she said, briskly nudging us awake. "We're going for a walk." We squeezed out of the pen, leaving lumps of wool on the wire, and followed her up the hill.

There are places all the darker for the nearness of the light. All around was deep ditch-black, and as we climbed, we saw the sky grow acid from the glow of the town far beyond the rise.

When we were younger, we often wondered at the strange behaviour of stars. They would appear suddenly in the distance, and move smoothly down a hill, vanish into its side and burst out somewhere else entirely. As they grew closer they would split into twins. Then we'd hear the growing burr of an engine, and a Ford Escort would speed past at the foot of the brae.

Here, at the top of the hill, overlooking the distant farmhouse, we saw a new star. This one appeared in the usual way, growing larger and brighter until we had to turn away. But this time, there was no discernible engine. And no twin. And it seemed to be right beside us.

Star-shadows stretched along the ground behind us, tying dark giants to our feet. And down below, like coughs of smoke from a chimney, the rest of the flock were climbing up towards us, in single file, picked out by the blinkless brilliance of the angel. For angel it was. And it spoke.

"Be not afraid!"

I ask you. The message was so at odds with the thundering messenger that we paid little attention. Our legs quivered as our terror plopped to the grass.

"I bring you good tidings of great joy!" it said. Silence. Who were we to argue? We waited.

"Unto you a child is born. But the child shall know no father nor mother, for its father shall be God."

The word rang out across the valley, tattering in the wind. Still we waited.

The angel seemed frustrated at the lack of feedback, and sent a flourish of lightning down towards the farmhouse. We murmured appreciatively. And waited.

"That's it," said the angel. "Show's over. Must dash."

"Wait!" came the shout from behind – my mother, ever practical. "To whom are you speaking?" she asked, judging formal speech best for this type of occasion.

My sister and I stood at the front, trembling equally in the angel glare, identical, indistinguishable, unmarked lambs for Fate to doom and Destiny to groom however they chose.

Sadly for my sister and her casseroled future, a butterfly stamped its foot.

It happened two years ago, in the suburbs of Tashkent, where the sun hammered down on a dusty market.

It didn't make much impact at the time, but it set off a chain reaction in the swirls and eddies of the planetary winds which, by the time it reached the Cheviots, was enough to flick a mote of grit into my right eye. I blinked, momentarily distracted, twitched a leg, skidded in the soft droppings at my feet and slid spectacularly towards the booming light.

"Behold," said the angel. "The favoured one."

And so it came to pass.

My daughter slithers from my sticky tube to a hail of flashing bulbs. I beam with surrogate parental pride at the Lamb of God, blinking my blood from her eyes. Born of no father, born of no mother, despite her rent-free tenancy of my womb. She looks nothing like me, with her mild white face. So who does she look like? Not like her father or mother – for she has neither, poor lamb.

No, she looks like herself. In fact, she is herself. She is exactly the same Finn Dorset ewe that was born six years ago, now born again, risen from the dead, revived from one tit cell taken from a laboratory fridge. The same ewe eaten by Mr Wright, the scientist, at a barbecue in 1993, where a burr hitched a lift on his cardie and a crow laid a clutch of freckled eggs.

Hello, Dolly. Nice to have you back.

Acknowledgements

Small Blue Thing won First Prize in the *Story Cellar* short story competition. It was dramatised for radio by the author, and broadcast on BBC Radio Scotland in a Bona Broadcasting production directed by Rosie Kellagher. It also appears on the *Eildon Tree* audio CD, *Eildon Leaves,* in a reading by the author.

Agnus Dei was shortlisted for *The Macallan/Scotland on Sunday* Short Story Competition and appears in the anthology *Shorts v.1.*

Life Kit #1 was shortlisted for the Fish Short Story Competition and appears in the anthology *Franklin's Grace.*

The Christmas Chair was broadcast on BBC Radio Scotland in a reading by Julie Austin, directed by David Ian Neville.

Bill McLaren Was My PE Teacher appeared in *Eildon Tree* magazine and was produced for the stage by Rowan Tree Theatre.

Quite The Thing was published in *New Writing Scotland 17: Friends and Kangaroos*.

Reinventing the Beach and *The Case Against Wings* were published in *Chapman* magazine. They were written during a Robert Louis Stevenson Fellowship residency in Grez-sur-Loing, France, supported by the National Library of Scotland.

Radar Bird was shortlisted for the Macallan/Scotland on Sunday competition and published in *Shorts v. 5*.

Wrapped Town and *Report* were published in *Eildon Tree* magazine.

Disinfected Youth and *Holiday Home* appeared in *Product* magazine as part of the *Particle Fiction* series.

A script version of *Pawkie Paiterson's Auld Grey Yaud* was performed by the Traverse Theatre at the Scotch Malt Whisky Society during the Edinburgh Festival Fringe.

About the Author

JULES HORNE IS from the Scottish Borders, and studied German and French at Oxford University. She has written over a dozen plays for BBC radio and the professional stage, and won many writing awards, including two Scotsman Edinburgh Fringe Firsts for ALLOTMENT (2011) and THREAD (2012), and the National Library of Scotland's RL Stevenson Fellowship. Jules has a background in radio journalism, and teaches creative writing for the Open University.

If you'd like to receive updates on future titles, please email info@juleshorne.com.

Nanonovels

Ever suffered from writer's block?

Jules Horne had a chronic form of the condition, known as writer's *lock*. Could a scientific experiment be the cure? She decided to write A STORY A DAY. IN FIVE MINUTES.

150 particle fictions, prose poems and nanodramas about eagles, trolls, Oulipo, Taylor's Theorem, Walden, sylosis, dogs, bumfles, leeches, toasted diamonds and other unexpected inspirations.

Visit www.juleshorne.com/nanonovels to find out more.

Lightning Source UK Ltd.
Milton Keynes UK
UKOW02f1820030616

275566UK00001B/12/P

9 780993 435430